Original Prin
A NOVEL

RANDY BOYAGODA

A JOHN METCALF BOOK

BIBLIOASIS
WINDSOR, ONTARIO

FIRST EDITION

Library and Archives Canada Cataloguing in Publication

Boyagoda, Randy, 1976-, author
    Original prin / Randy Boyagoda.

Issued in print and electronic formats.
ISBN 978-1-77196-245-2 (softcover).--ISBN 978-1-77196-246-9 (ebook)

    I. Title.

PS8603.O9768O75 2018   C813'.6   C2018-901728-7
                                             C2018-901729-5

Edited by John Metcalf
Copy Edited by Emily Donaldson
Cover Design by Michel Vrana
Typeset by Chris Andrechek

Published with the generous assistance of the Canada Council for the Arts, which last year invested $153 million to bring the arts to Canadians throughout the country, and the financial support of the Government of Canada. Biblioasis also acknowledges the support of the Ontario Arts Council (OAC), an agency of the Government of Ontario, which last year funded 1,709 individual artists and 1,078 organizations in 204 communities across Ontario, for a total of $52.1 million, and the contribution of the Government of Ontario through the Ontario Book Publishing Tax Credit and the Ontario Media Development Corporation.

Author acknowledgments: Thank you to John Metcalf, Dan Wells, Kim Witherspoon, Charles Foran, and T.H. Adamowski. I also gratefully acknowledge the support I received for writing this book from Ryerson University, the University of St. Michael's College, the University of Toronto, and from the Glen Workshop in Santa Fe, New Mexico. Chapter 17 originally appeared in *Commonweal* magazine.

PRINTED AND BOUND IN CANADA

For Anna,
and for Mira, Olive, Ever, and Imogen:
My originals in life and love

"Perhaps in you is the sense that citizens of Canada
are not involved in the real root of the threat."
—David Foster Wallace, *Infinite Jest*

Part One

1

EIGHT MONTHS BEFORE he became a suicide bomber, Prin went to the zoo with his family. Puffy and brightly balaclava'd, the six of them fanned across an empty parking lot. Ahead of them was a billboard advertising the zoo's newest additions. Two furry gifts from China snuggled in the smiling Prime Minister's lap, chewing bamboo shoots that pointed in perilous directions. Prin experienced a sympathetic twinge in his own groin. This was the day to tell them.

"The baby panda bears are turning into polar bears!" said his six-year-old, Maisie.

"That's just snow sticking to the picture," said his ten-year-old, Philomena.

"That's called climate change," said his eight-year-old, Chiara.

"I won't eat them!" said his four-year-old, Pippa.

"Who wants a snack?" asked his wife, Molly.

He strode out in front, the family food bag slung across his back.

It was lunchtime, and they hadn't eaten since more or less an hour before the Mass they'd attended at a plaster-walled church on the rusty eastern edge of the city. The church was fronted by chipped saints' shrines and wedges of stumpy evergreen shrubs. Everything was fretted in winter road salt. The church was surrounded by an endless run of ethnic food stores and hair salons and paycheque-advance shops, by mid-rise apartments and crime-scene hotels and diners for old white people.

Inside, almost everyone was poor and South Asian. Prin's own parents had come from Sri Lanka in the 1960s. His father had worked downtown, eighty hours a week, and raised him far from the city, in a suburban paradise of flavoured coffee and televisions in every bedroom and streets named for fruit and kings and there were no other brown people.

Whereas at a church like St. Teresa's, in deep Scarborough, the people went to communion in sincere moustaches and dark, dismal suits, in wedding gold and bright crimson saris that flowed into snow boots. The little girls wore braids past their waists. The boys wore quickly hemmed dress pants over Lebron James-endorsed basketball shoes. Everyone had sideburns. Everyone was singing folk hymns to Mother Mary and her baby, songs that cut to the heart.

He took his family to this church once a year, on January 1, in an aging Volvo with a trunk full of emergency supplies—road flares, iPad chargers, unread *New Yorkers*—and also the gingham grocery store bag he was now carrying into the zoo as his family debated pandas and polar bears behind him, his wife asking him to slow down so everyone could have a snack.

The bag was packed with bananas and avocados and also a St. Sebastian's cranberry-spelt loaf Molly had baked that morning. At the bottom of the bag was a champagne-foiled sparkling-juice bottle, which, in keeping with family tradition, they'd brought to toast the lemurs on New Year's Day.

Which was, this year, also the day to tell them.

This was why they had come, in spite of the weather and Prin's father calling in the morning to remind him that the Chinese now owned Volvo. Would you trust the lives of your children to car tires made by Falun Gong prisoners? To car tires probably made *of* Falun Gong prisoners?

His father was divorced, had sold his convenience store in the inner city to a condo developer, subscribed to a premium alternative-news package, and had a lot of time to think and forward emails.

Prin and Molly had decided to stop calling it just a potty problem. He was going in for surgery later that January. The plan was to take the girls to one of the more obscure exhibits and explain it there and leave it there, in a place they would never visit again.

Girls, something awful is growing inside your daddy. It's called cancer, and it looks like this:

Mole rats: blind, pink, splotchy, writhing, they lived in a stacked complex of glass tubes. Their lives were spent crawling and squeezing over each other, their dull, plump shapes pulsing and proliferating in low light. Who wouldn't want a very careful doctor with a super-powerful robot assistant to cut all of these gross and pointless bodies out of their beloved zoo, their beloved daddy?

They would ask: When they cut it out, would he bleed like when he was shaving and yelling that they were late for church? What does prostate cancer look like? Does it bite?

The forums he'd visited recommended finding something like mole rats when it was time to tell the kids. An Evangelical from Naperville, Illinois posted that he drove his kids to the parking lot of a mosque in South Side Chicago to tell them. An hour later, he posted that Islam is a religion of peace. While the others debated, Prin image-searched zoo animals until he found the blind mole rats of Toronto.

But they never made it. Shortly after entering the zoo, wet snow began to wallop them. The children decided to take a break from all the walking just as they reached the first concession stand.

"Oh please Daddy, can we have some chocolates?" asked Chiara.

"You just had some," said Prin.

"That was all the way back in the car ride! Also, these are … traditional Santa Claus boots full of Belgian-chocolate reindeer droppings," said Maisie.

Despite the snow smacking them around, everyone stopped to congratulate Maisie on her reading. Maisie now looked meaningfully at her older sisters, who immediately proposed chocolates so that the entire family could celebrate her dramatic advances in literacy.

"I want to eat reindeer droppings! You never let me eat reindeer droppings!" said Pippa.

"Mom, they're on sale," said Philomena.

"Not just on sale. They're on deep discount. Maisie, what's 75 percent off $12.99?" asked Chiara.

"Chiara, why don't you tell us the answer," said Molly.

"That's like, like, like, wait, I know, please, Mom, WAIT—"

"Let's go, girls, and we'll work on your math at home, Chiara," said Molly.

Defeated, the children were easier to push ahead. The family paid a fast visit to the African rhinoceros standing all by herself in a snow-covered concrete savannah in far-eastern Toronto; she was wondering what the hell her parents were thinking when they decided to move to Canada.

They made for the nearest indoor space. The butterfly hall was so humid that the snow-doused children began melting and sweating and crying for help to tear off their soaking balaclavas even before they passed through the thick plastic strips that kept the butterflies in their optimal subtropical climate. Prin headed back outside and looked up through the pelting swirls.

The midday sky was now pewter and thunder shook out from behind the bare trees.

Could this be a sign?

Was God using a winter weather event to tell him this was the perfect day to tell the girls, or was He telling him to go home and keep them safe from bad roads and bad news? The sky also went dark and thunder sounded while Christ hung on the cross. But other than his mother, who would take him seriously for making that connection? He was no Christ. He was a forty-year-old associate professor of English with early-stage prostate cancer.

"Maybe we should just go home," Prin said.

"Whatever you think is best, dear," Molly said.

But she always said that. Did she always mean it? After twelve years of marriage and now with this diagnosis and this snowed-out plan to tell the children, it felt to Prin too late, or too early, to find out.

"LEMURS! DADDY! WE CAN'T GO HOME YET! WE NEED TO TOAST THE LEMURS!"

2

PRIN WAS SURPRISED to find other people in the lemur house. He wouldn't have told them in here anyway, but he'd been hoping, given the weather, that they would have at least had the place to themselves. Instead, two university-age Asian girls with metallic brown hair in matching bowl cuts sat on a bench across from the animals' glassed-in enclosure, studying their phones.

There was also a family from out of town. The parents wore unendorsed running shoes and shapeless blue jeans. The dad had a neck beard and a bright blue, straight-billed Blue Jays cap that he wore in reverse. He was drinking from a giant bottle of bright purple Gatorade. The mom had spiky short hair and was chewing gum, dramatically. They were bickering over what looked like a flip phone. They had three children—little twin boys with rat-tails running around with robot figurines, and an older girl with purplish hair who was standing off to the side with a novel Prin recognized from that year's community-reading exercise at his university. The book was a national bestseller about corruption-fighting vampires who were also Indigenous youth leaders.

"Okay, girls, finish your snacks. Don't take off your coats. We're not staying long. Let's find the New Year lemur and have our toast," Prin said.

He pulled the sparkling juice from his bag.

"We got Iron Mans for Christmas!" the little boys said, leaning into him, trying to see what else was in the food bag.

"JAYDEN! BRAYDEN! Get over here. Hey, who wants iPad?" said the other father.

By the time Prin had very carefully, even ritually un-foiled the bottle and set up the little glasses, his own children were crowded around the other family's twins, all of them jockeying for more screen. Molly was chatting with the other mom and nodding commiseratively.

"Looks like it's just you and me for the bottle, eh buddy?" said the other father.

"Sorry? Oh yeah, right," said Prin.

His heart was now beating hard with the sudden effort of remembering, in addition to the remarks he planned to deliver to his children about his cancer diagnosis, that day's college football games and the names of the different kinds of saws he owned and how many cylinders were in his car's engine.

Wait. Was it pistons?

"So, what are we drinking?" the other father asked.

"Sparkling juice. Nothing alcoholic, sorry. It's kind of a thing we do every New Year's Day. We come to the zoo and raise a toast to the lemurs," said Prin.

"Yeah, my kids loved that Disney movie too. Which one was it again?" asked the other father.

"Sorry, I'm not sure," he said.

Prin was lying. But that was better than what he wanted to do, which was tell this man in a baseball cap that his own children loved the Royal Zoological Society of London vintage print hanging in their bedroom, their nursery. He wanted to remark that lemurs were famously curious and creative animals. Prin liked to think his family was curious and creative, too. Mindful that it might not be as readily apparent to his wife and children, he had provided Molly and the girls with various explanations of the connection he saw between lemurs and their family.

They humoured him, mostly by letting him believe he was humouring them.

"I can't believe I can't remember the name of that movie either! We even had it going on both screens in the van when we drove here!" the other father said.

"So you're from out of town?"

"Huh? Oh, yeah. The library gives out free passes. Ours expired yesterday but we took a shot and it worked out. And we had a pretty late night, if you know what I mean, so I figured just bring the kids here and let them run around while I drink fifty gallons of Gatorade, right? It's all about the kids, anyway, right? Even if I'm missing—"

"Oklahoma-Notre Dame!" Prin said.

"Wait, crap, you think we're going to be stuck here until 8 o'clock? Maybe, eh? This weather's right fierce. They were calling it Snowpocalypse on the news. Buddy, the best decision CNN ever made was giving Trump his own 24-hour weather show after all that stuff happened and he got fired or fired himself or whatever. I still don't understand that situation. Do you?" the other dad asked.

"Well, if you were to ask Theodor Adorno—"

"Who's he play for, Notre Dame?" the other dad asked.

"He was, well, a thinker about the culture," said Prin.

"Which culture?" the other dad asked.

"Actually that's a good question—"

"Hundred percent. And it's all about everyone needing to have the right phone, right? Anyways, you got four kids, eh? All girls? Still trying for the boy, right? I hear that. After we had the twins, I got the snip. I'm Shane, by the way. What's your name? What are you, some kind of doctor? I know this guy from Bangla—, wait, I think he's from Bangla-something. Hey Alanna, where's Jag-ditch from again? It starts Bangla—"

Suddenly there was a loud snapping noise and the lights went out. Through one of the big windows you could see sparks jumping up and around. They were coming out of a black cable flailing around on the snow-covered ground.

"Cool, Daddy, look!" one of Prin's daughters said.

Everyone went to the window. Shane and Alanna fussed over a small digital camera while their boys' kept slamming their Iron Mans against the glass. They were desperate to get outside and ride the wire, fight the wire, aim the wire, fire the wire. Standing behind Molly and the girls, Prin watched the cable sparking pointlessly. Molly reached for his hand and squeezed it and smiled. She was fine with their living as brother and sister for the rest of their lives. What mattered was having rest of their lives.

Prin agreed. He had to agree. How could he not agree? But still. Prin smiled and squeezed back and continued to ache, pointlessly.

What would Adorno do?

Now they were all standing in the dark, staring out at a grey storm that had turned into thick, pinning rain. In the sudden quiet that even the children observed, you could really hear it hammering on the roof of the lemur house.

Prin wondered what they were doing in there, the lemurs. Were they still swinging around on knotty, low-slung ropes, or were they lolling on their thick rubber furniture, peeling oranges and napping and snuggling themselves with their own tails and making his daughters wish they could live like lemurs too? Were those glossy black eyes tracking everything the whole time? Were they pondering why no one was toasting them, or trying to figure out who was dropping all those marbles and nails on their sudden nighttime sky?

When was he supposed to tell the children?

There had been a plan, a good plan, a prayed-about and well-researched plan. He felt cheated. He had long since accepted the fear and the pain that had come with his diagnosis. He knew this was real. He also knew that what was real for him was small compared to what was real fear and pain for so many others. But he knew it was real too, his portion. And all he wanted from God and the world was five minutes with his kids in front of some blind mole rats. They had defied the Trumpian weather and the Chinese tires and come to the zoo and the plan had fallen apart. What did God expect him to do, instead? Tell them tomorrow?

That wasn't the plan!

If he did what he really wanted to do, had wanted to do for so very long, which was scream and scream and scream, what would happen next?

"E-cigarettes don't give much light. Anyone bring candles?" Shane asked.

When he was a boy, Prin would demand that God prove He was truly there in church by making the candles on the altar flicker. Then, going back and forth between hope and terror and feeling vindicated both ways, he would close his eyes for long stretches. He never told anyone about his chancing with God like this. If he did, some grown-up would have ruined the whole thrilling, secret dare of it.

He didn't know what, but he knew it was more than merely a child's game. He knew this was true from when he was very small, because of the final time his father had taken him to pick up his mother from where she worked. Prin sat beside daddy on the front seat of the big blue Caprice. Daddy kept his arm around him the whole time they drove, using the other to steer and smoke and point out all the birds and cars in the world.

Then one day, while they were waiting in the parking lot, a baldy man came to their window. He tapped and Daddy opened it. Cold wind came in first. It must have been winter. The baldy man put his hands on the open frame of the car door. He had a funny yellow bracelet on his wrist. He put his head into their car, and he screamed at them for a long time. He screamed and screamed and screamed. No words. It was like he was standing on frying pans. Then the baldy man leaned out, let go of their car, turned, and went and sat on the concrete steps leading to the front doors of the hospital.

Daddy had his arm around Prin the whole time but Prin only noticed now that it was shaking. Then he said, "Wait here, son. I will come back," and he got out of the car and went over to the man sitting on the steps. He leaned in on him and screamed. He screamed for much longer than the man had screamed at them, then turned and came back to the car. The man never looked up. Two nurses wearing white hats meant for French fries came out and took him away. Then his mother stopped working at the funny hospital and got a job at the regular hospital.

What did it mean if the candles didn't flicker? What if they went out? And never mind what it meant. What would happen if they didn't flicker? Was that why that baldy man was yelling? Had he already figured it all out? Was he trying to tell them? But the baldy man was wrong! Whenever Prin peeked during Mass, there they were, the candles. And this was, for Prin the boy, sufficient proof of the existence of God.

Prin the man knew he was supposed to know better but still, when he wasn't preventing his children from executing hip hop moves between the pews at Mass, he still dared those candles. Only now, in this dark zoo of his life, there weren't even any candles to dare.

Then everyone got a text.

It was from the zoo itself, informing patrons in the lemur house that due to unsafe conditions, they were to remain where they were until further notice. Emergency personnel had been contacted and were en route. Backup generators would be activated shortly.

3

THIRTY MINUTES LATER, the children began screaming as a
monster came out of the dark. The back-up generator cleared
its throat and grumbled to life. The place warmed up fast,
and the moms took everyone's wet gear and hung it all to dry
on the corners of information boards flashing error messages.
The Asian girls conferred and left, smiling and nodding their
way past Shane and Prin's attempts to stop them.

So now it was just the two families. Within an hour the iPad
was dead; an hour later the phones were, too. Soon all the games
and songs and snacks and ghost stories were finished.

They toasted the lemurs as a family—as two families. Prin's
girls scooted and crouched along the glass, waving and beckoning, popping up and down, their faces bright and urgent.

Who could get a lemur to look first?

Who would pick the New Year's lemur this time?

Only they stayed away, the lemurs. They turned in on
themselves and peeked at the people over coils of tail and the
furry backs of family members. The twins were banging on the
glass with their action figures and calling out threats that were
shouted down by Shane's demand that his older daughter join
in the fun and then by his own cajoling and banging on the glass
with his camouflage-coated e-cigarette. Never mind his cur-
dling soul, Prin's heart belled when he saw how his daughters

placed their hands on the boys' wrists to make them drop the Iron Mans.

The three older girls calmed the boys and showed them how much better it was to be soft, quiet, gentle. Little Pippa reached up to do the same to Shane, who stepped back like a giant backing away from a hummingbird made of spun sugar.

Now all six children were bright and urgent and pantomiming along the enclosure. Soon furry heads began to pop up and linger. Curious, the lemurs began to advance. One called out and the sound was like a comedian impersonating a monkey impersonating a loon. Dart and stop, dart and stop and turn, dart and stop and go on, they came closer and closer, their big eyes panning up at their hard-pinging heavens.

"Daddy, look, I think that little one on the side is looking at me!" said one of the boys.

"You picked the New Year lemur!" said Philomena.

The children cheered. Shane cursed the battery in his camera, which had died unexpectedly. Prin could find nothing sour or false in his daughters' cheering, in these other people taking what should have been theirs. He felt rebuked and rebuked.

"I think you should talk to Shane," Molly said.

Still more rebuked.

"About what?" asked Prin.

"Alanna had breast cancer. It's in remission now," Molly said.

"Oh. Is that what you were talking about, before the power went out?" asked Prin.

"Yes, and he might have some advice about how to tell the kids," Molly said.

"Molly, I have a plan for how to tell the kids, remember?" said Prin.

"I know, dear, but it doesn't look like it's going to work out. Anyway, she said Shane had a really good idea for how to do it," Molly said.

"So, you told her about me, about the diagnosis," Prin said.

"We were just talking about how we're both always just so tired, and I must have mentioned it," Molly said.

"So yes, you told her," Prin said.

Molly made a pained face.

"Molly," he said.

"The children know something's wrong. You need to tell them. Your surgery's only a few weeks away. And they can tell I'm worried about something, about you, but I've said nothing because I know you're trying to be careful and thoughtful with the news. Only the plan's not working out the way you wanted. So do something else. Talk to Shane. Or play with the kids while you can. Do something else. Don't just stand here looking at your dead phone."

He waited for her to start crying, but this time she didn't; she didn't offer to split a Hail Mary and she didn't wait around for a hug, either.

They had met in a church basement in Milwaukee in the early 2000s. At the time, Molly was an undergraduate at Marquette. She lived at home and was volunteering with a Montessori program. Prin was a graduate student from Toronto who spent one morning a week at a soup kitchen helping old men read *Sports Illustrated*. Secretly, he liked the way they talked about food and women. He could never. Volunteering gave a little moral ballast to the hours and hours he spent reading and talking about reading and writing about talking and reading.

The two of them met a few days after Prin had broken up with his graduate-school girlfriend, who was five years older than he was, didn't want children, and didn't really eat food. She was sort of Jewish, and from New York City And everyone always thought Prin was a good little Catholic boy from Canada. This would show them!

The entire time Prin had dated his graduate-school girlfriend he willed himself to believe that the life ahead of them, when they got married, or did whatever you did instead of getting married, was what he wanted. At friends' parties in hot apartments full of ferns and cats named Sontag and Mephistopheles, she liked to say that they were the ironic Abelard and Heloise: he was a celibate who wasn't a priest, and she was a none who was no nun, the homonym being the joke that led into a discussion of her dissertation research into sexual wordplay in popular women's magazines.

She was small and bony and post-everything, including monogamy, as Prin was shown in the worst possible way one afternoon.

Whereas Molly was beautiful and round and baked every day and was everything Catholic and Catholic everything, and they married inside a year and he got a job back in Toronto and after four children and a three-bedroom house and two lines of credit and one positive diagnosis, their life together had been good and was good. Like skating on a river. You hear what might be cracks but what's the good of thinking about them? It's good, even great, so long as you keep going.

Had been, was, and would be good, great: it was only prostate cancer! And early stage, no less! This was not *cancer* cancer. He certainly knew the difference. We all do. A school friend's father, an uncle, a few of Molly's aunts, assorted neighbours and godparents: all suddenly wasting and suddenly bald but grinning for pictures, and then wasted and bony and glancing off-camera, and then, now, gone.

Whereas this was Prin's cancer: he had trouble going to the bathroom for a while and then he wet his pants without noticing at a neighbour's backyard party. And now he had to tell them. And he had had a really good plan, a plan that was prayed-about and well-researched—he wasn't screaming and screaming and screaming like he could have been.

What more could God ask of him?

"Excuse me, Shane, can I get your advice about something?" Prin asked.

4

SHANE AND ALANNA told their kids she had breast cancer by driving all the way to downtown Toronto, paying twenty bucks for parking, and then sitting down to a sushi dinner. Shane had looked at the same website that Prin had.

"They were crying anyway because of that green Wahhabi stuff you put on it, so that's how we told them," said Shane.

"Wasabi," said Prin.

"Killer for sure! It totally works! Good luck to you in your situation, buddy, you got some great girls. They're so smart! I don't know half the words they're saying! And I'm cutting my goatee and stuff back to rock a moustache for you next Mo'vember, hundred percent. You're going to beat this. You should friend me so I can show you my 'stache," said Shane.

"Thanks, Shane," Prin said.

They fist-bumped.

Shane cleared his throat and cracked his neck left, then right.

"Look, can I give you some advice?" Shane asked.

"Sure," Prin said.

"Life is highway, right? But at some point, we all hit a deer. And what do you hope?" Shane asked.

"I'm not sure," Prin said.

"You hope you hit a fawn, or at least a doe. Not too much damage, and if you can field-dress by the side of the road, you got a freezer full of meat for your trouble. That's the best situation. What's the worst?" Shane asked.

"Hitting a moose?" Prin asked.

Shane stepped back like someone had spattered paint in his face. He blinked violently.

"Whoa. I never thought of that. I guess the moose is like, well, death, right?" Shane asked.

Both men went quiet.

"I need to go back and think about that one, buddy. But anyway, I don't think you're in a hitting-a-moose situation with prostate cancer. It's more like you've hit a buck. That's where I was going. Fawn and doe, okay, but a buck? Let's say you hit a buck. Wait, are you still following me?" Shane asked.

"Yes," Prin said.

"So hitting a buck's not death, but it's a lot of damage, right? And you can sort of give up or you can still get something out of the situation. And here's the thing. It's buckmeat. You ever eat buckmeat?" Shane asked.

"No," Prin said.

"It's tough. Like life right now, living with cancer," Shane said.

"Indeed," Prin said.

"So that's where your girls get the fancy words from!" Shane said.

"Daddy, come see! It's raining on the lemurs!" one of the girls said.

Moments later, a branch came down on the see-through ceiling of the lemur house. Panels gave way and fell with a great crash of broken glass and ice. The branch itself dangled and dripped down through the opening. The lemurs stared up at the rain now pouring straight down into their world.

Now where was that coming from?

And what was this new black-and-green climb-me that had poked through and now was beckoning?

One of them was creative and curious enough to climb up and find out. It grabbed onto a long, thick rope leading from one play structure to the next and swung towards the sudden opening in the heavens, ignoring all the humans below banging on the viewing glass and screaming that it wasn't worth it.

Glancing back from the hard weather, the lemur paused, then scooted up and slipped out. Prin ran to the door to block the children from going outside to save the lemur and from there saw a furry black ball fall back inside. Everyone screamed, then cheered: the lemur had caught hold of a rope and saved its own life!

Happy New Year!

He was going to beat cancer!

He would tell them right now.

He made his way over to Molly and the girls, but before he could reach them there was more banging on the glass and pleading, because the lemur wasn't curious or creative. It was just a trapped animal. It climbed up again, scrambling along the black, wet bark of the fallen branch. A new rope slipped down beside it.

It grabbed the new rope. Only this time, it wasn't a rope.

The lemur falls a second time.

The lemur shrieked and shrieked before letting go of the broken wire and falling a very long way, pinwheeling a little. It landed near the glass and ice. The sound was loud, sudden, over. They couldn't actually see the body because all the other lemurs had gathered around to grieve, or maybe they were just curious. Prin walked over to his own grieving and freaked-out family. Shane gave him two thumbs up and nodded.

They'd never come to the lemur house again.

And what a small price that was to pay, Prin thought. He suddenly felt a tremor of love, of being loved and cared for well past his knowing, all of them loved and cared for well beyond themselves. They weren't curious and creative and trapped and fallen animals. They each of them counted for far more than lemurs and sparrows. There could be no better time or place to tell them. He had trusted only in himself! How trapped and false and grasping he had been! God had a greater plan than any one of Prin's, and now, at last, in His Mercy—

"Girls! Listen up! Your dad's got cancer of the privates. But don't worry, he's totally going to kill this buck! I believe in him! You have to believe in him! We all have to believe in him!"

"Thanks, Shane," said Prin.

"Indeed. Hey who's using the fancy words now, right?"

They fist-bumped, a second time.

5

EARLY FEBRUARY: FROM his hospital window Prin could see red and green bars of holdover holiday light travelling up and down the CN Tower, and also the paper-white panes of office glass and the yellow beacons that tipped the endless construction cranes cranked up around the city. What a prosperous, busy, starry heavens was Toronto just then!

Molly and the girls had left a few hours before, as had his parents. His surgery was scheduled for 6 am. He should have gone to bed, or read something spiritual, or written a letter to the children. But what could he possibly say? He loved them, and this is what he loved about them, about each of them, and this is what he would miss. The thought of it was terrifying. To name such things, just in case. Terrifying.

He should have written to Molly. He owed her an apology. He owed her many apologies. The one that, well, weighed most heavily upon him just then concerned a very small, very hard little nailhead of a secret. For months Prin had wondered if Molly was just a little to blame for his getting prostate cancer. From the beginning of their marriage, she had fallen asleep every night with one of her big, beautiful legs draped across his small, bony midriff. How was that even comfortable for her? He slipped it off when he could tell she was sleeping, except during Lent, when he treated the loving burden, while not exactly as heavy as a cross upon the shoulder, as an opportunity for solidarity with Christ.

Prin once told a priest as much during confession, as part of a larger reflection on the paradox of prideful humility. The priest listened to Prin go on and on and then said he was pretty sure that if Molly had to listen to this kind of thing from her husband, she was the one who was suffering in solidarity with Christ.

But over the years couldn't something have been bent, crushed, moved around, metastasized? Late night searching suggested there were no studies of this, because what kind of husband would ever volunteer such information to a doctor?

He wouldn't apologize to Molly because then she'd know what he'd been thinking and every night, for the rest of their lives, there'd be that moment when she turned to him and then stopped herself and he would wonder if she were lying beside him in rage or sadness, neither of which she deserved. None of a certain sub-basement portion of Prin's thoughts did Molly deserve, probably going all the way back to that church basement in Milwaukee, when he saw her and knew she was perfect, the perfect opposite of his ex-girlfriend, and he decided, very quickly, that that could be enough.

Prin gathered up the folds of his hospital sheets in his hands and crushed them, wishing these awful thoughts were in these sheets, crushed and suffocating. Just like his prostate had likely been crushed and suffocated for years on end in his marital bed.

NO! Molly was neither perfect, nor anyone else's perfect opposite, nor the cause of his cancer. Molly was good and true and beautiful in her way and had quietly and efficiently and obligingly given him such a life, such a good life. His salary as a professor at a small downtown university was considerable, were he a priest or nun from the 1950s. For a twenty-first-century city family, it was just enough; Molly extended the lives of running shoes and rubber bands across four small girls. She did this without complaint. Sometimes Prin worried not just that he treated Molly and their marriage as a lifelong morality play, but that she knew it, too. He never considered that she did the same, only that she deserved better than him and his thoughts.

If he died, Prin wanted her to marry a lawyer or insurance executive with a strong, broad midriff, a man capable of carrying such love and knowing it only as love. And if he lived, Prin resolved that after the surgery he would do better by his wife.

His heart stirred.

That was all and only what was needed, all that was already good and true and beautiful about his life, and it would begin and end there, with loving her. Prin decided to sleep in the peace of this knowledge and then to get on with things, whether he woke to bright lights or Bright Light. He sighed, made the sign of the cross, and slept.

He sat up and checked his email. He liked the idea of waking to a clean inbox, or going on to eternity with no one waiting for a reply. There were a series of FWD FWD PLS DON'T DELETE messages from his mother reporting on the holy legions of village women praying for him in Sri Lanka. His father sent him links to various miracle cures for impotence that featured certain kinds of fruit and specific sleeping positions. His high-school buddies sent him Viagra offers and his sisters, who lived overseas, sent him emoji-fretted scans of the crayoned Get Well cards their kids had made for him. He was also cc'd on a remarkably long string of remarkably detailed messages exchanged by moms from the kids' school. These set out action plans, complete with workflow charts and recommended scheduling apps, for providing the family with meals during Prin's recuperation.

There were many messages from his colleagues at the university, who emailed him prayers and thoughts and good thoughts and best wishes and good vibes and positive vibes. A professor of corporate social responsibility promised to share her personal mindfulness space with him until he recovered. She also promised to send him an advance copy of her new book. She wanted nothing in return, only that he someday pay it forward. If Prin wanted to put it on a future syllabus, that was totally up to him. She could give a talk and even waive her honorarium, but obviously that could be discussed later. She'd send him her PowerPoint as well, just in case. Anyway, main thing was to get better, be mindful, and pay it forward!

Prin was also assured by the president of the university, Fr. Pat, that everyone was on the journey to healing with him and also that his responsibilities, when he returned to campus, would be restricted to light administrative duties. Meanwhile, Fr. Pat encouraged Prin to keep up with life on campus by reading his blog, *Metaphysical Therapy*. Finally, Fr. Pat shared an excerpt from a sermon by a fourth-century Irish preacher that he hoped would offer some consolation ("And no, he's not my uncle … I'm not that old, LOL!").

The religion of souls should follow the law of the development of bodies. If, however, the human form were to turn into some shape that did not belong to its own nature, or even if something were added to the sum of its members or subtracted from it, the whole body would necessarily perish or become grotesque or at least be enfeebled. But never your soul, Jane!

Pax and Warm Blessings, Pat

The white-headed old man could have at least cut and paste Prin's name in place of the last cancer patient he wrote. But Prin shook for a moment at the thought of how many such messages even a university priest must send. Who was Jane? Was she still alive? He offered her a Hail Mary. She definitely hadn't died of prostate cancer.

Nor would Prin. He was certainly on the younger side for it but he had earned a low Gleason score. Only one in every forty men with a score that low died inside ten years of diagnosis, Google had assured him, and then his smooth Asian urologist told him, "Your glandular architecture is presenting as only moderately abnormal at this point in the cancer staging." And now, a few months later, he would indeed have something subtracted from his body, a part of his member subtracted from his member.

His grad-school ex-girlfriend, now a professor of English and Strategic Thinking at a college in Montana (according to his most recent casual late night searching) would have loved the punny poetic justice of this neo-Abelardian fate. He didn't Google her very often. Only when he was, well, not bored, and not longing for anything in particular, but just wondering, *What if?* Would he, with her, be living childless and cat- and fern-filled, in Montana? Not waking up to small voices, laughing and calling. Not going to bed in softness, full of pie. He didn't Google her this time. He just turned off his phone.

He looked outside again. The Prime Minister was on another billboard, this time snuggling two little bald black children in need of Canada's help.

He turned on his phone. He reread the sermon Fr. Pat had sent him. Yes, he would be enfeebled, though he had been assured by the hairless Asian surgeon that there would be nothing grotesque about it, only a small scar. The only grotesquerie, in fact, was what this diagnosis had done to his soul.

The news in recent days had been full, again, of baptisms and weddings blown apart in the Middle East, of men chopped down, of women and children leaving their homes to hide in Biblical mountains, and all of them on their knees, bowed down and veiled, heaving, gasping, praying and begging for help, mercy, food, water—for themselves, their children, their beloveds.

And if God didn't answer as they were hoping God would, then what, for them?

Nullity.

But he didn't really believe that. Only in this life would they have such nullity—bloody, flaming nullity—and then they would go home, *home,* into the mind of God. All of them, all of us, we are homeward so. We are known before we can know better, we are ashes and dust to blood and mud, mud and blood to ashes and dust, then Mind. Prin had long since been known and found and kept, and still was, and would always be. No matter what happened with the surgery, or what he did, and couldn't do afterwards. Suddenly a wire of light passed through him. *All will be well.* But it left a black streak behind.

Since his diagnosis, Prin had been thinking it wasn't fair. He didn't deserve this. He'd even blamed his wife. But really, he didn't deserve this luxury of lying around thinking about it. Only that this had been granted, and he should do something about it. He could, couldn't he?

Why in this life did he enjoy so much better a place in the mind of God than any of the poor people hiding in those old, holy mountains? Huddled behind a boulder, hearing a jeep with a black flag and bearded young men bristling with blades and guns hammering up the mountain pass, coming for you and your kids.

If he survived the surgery, Prin vowed he'd be a much better husband, and also do more with his life than support his family as one of the world's leading scholarly experts on representations of seahorses and other marine life in Canadian literature. He would do something worthy of all that God had granted him.

He slept.

6

PRIN LOOKED UP into the bright lights above the operating table. He could only look for so long before having to close his eyes. What should have been blackness behind those closed eyes was orangey-red, the amber of ember light. There was a radio playing ragtime music in the background, and doctors and nurses in masks were complaining about their phone plans. Which meant this was normal and all was well and all would be well. He was wrapped in a heated blanket and told to count down from ten, nine, eight, but he said Hail Marys until seven, slix, fi, fo Mary, fee of grace...

Deep, deep he went. He dreamt he was in a restaurant that only served seahorses. He stood at the hostess booth, giving a lecture. Refugee families kept coming in, asking about wait times for tables.

"He's awake!" one of the girls said.

"Daddy!" another of the girls said.

"Princely! My only beloved son! Praise Jesus!" Prin's mother Lizzie said.

"My wife's only beloved son! Praise Jesus and also all religions!" said Kareem, Lizzie's new Muslim husband.

"You, Molly, give him the rest of that Big Mac. He's hungry," Prin's father Kingsley said.

"Daddy, how do you go to the bathroom now?" another of the girls asked.

"Hi, love. The doctor told me the operation was successful. How are you feeling? Are you okay?" Molly said.

"Molly. I am. I love you," Prin said.

He began crying. A nurse explained this was a possible side effect of the anaesthesia, and through his tears Prin insisted the tears were real and tried to say why but just cried more. The nurse shrugged and went to get the doctor. Molly smiled and wiped his tears and was about to tell him that she—but by then the girls and Prin's mother had shouldered their way in between them, everyone sobbing except Prin's father and Prin's stepfather. The two older men were nearer the door, standing beside each other and not making eye contact.

He loved all of them, just then. He'd come through. He didn't even mind his new stepfather being there. His mother had met him, an Ismaili grocer, at his store, Kareem of the Crop. Kingsley made a poor big show of not being offended by Kareem's presence at family events. He also made a big show of passing a metal detector over his body every time he saw him. Lizzie boiled but Kareem laughed it off. After all, he drove a newer old Cadillac than his new wife's ex-husband, and with a vanity plate no less—GO2HLAL.

"Seriously, how do you go to the bathroom now?" Kareem asked.

Then, in a loud, discreet voice, Lizzie asked Prin if he needed her help ... "that way." She was already tugging at the sheets.

"The men of my family, stand up!" Prin's father said.

He then ordered the room cleared. He needed to speak with his son. He stalked the hospital room in his loafers and corduroys and Harris tweed jacket, arms behind his back, intensely studying an invisible line on the floor.

His family line, now.

Unless.

"Son," Kingsley said.

"Dad," Prin said.

"Son," Kingsley said.

"Dad," Prin said.

"Do you know how hard I worked, to give us this life in Canada? I came here with a suitcase and a transistor radio. How many televisions did you grow up with? More than most people have in brothers and sisters!" Kingsley said.

"Yes, Dad, thank you." Prin said. Again.

"And?" Kingsley asked.

"And thank you ... very much?" Prin said.

"NO! I didn't do all of that just so my last name would die on some operating table in Toronto," Kingsley said.

"Oh. Well Dad, I'm not sure there's anything to be done," Prin said.

"What if I'd thought that way fifty years ago in the British High Commissioner's Office in Colombo when the clerk informed me that my application to Canada had been misplaced? When he told me he wasn't sure there was anything to be done? Where would we be now?" Kingsley asked.

"In a hospital in Colombo, with the same situation?" Prin said.

"Of course not! You would have grown up eating real fruits and sleeping in traditional poses. Didn't you get my email? Whereas here you've been polluted by a rotten civilization. Apples on steroids and memory foam! But good news, son! I have a plan," Kingsley said.

"Dad—"

"I know, I know, first you have to get better. Listen, you don't have to worry about having more children. I am your father. I have a plan," Kingsley said.

What plan?

"What worries me is whether you'll be fully healed before the father-son pickleball tournament in April. I had her ask the doctor—"

"You mean Molly?" Prin said. Again.

"I know her name! I asked her to ask the doctor, and he said you'll be okay before then, before April, so you can play. You'll play, right?" Kingsley said.

"Yes, Dad, if I'm better by then," Prin said.

"Good. Now, the plan. I'm going to pay for you to go to Sri Lanka next summer. I will come with you. And we're going to visit the best healer in the village. You'll come back ready to start the family," Kingsley said.

"I already have four children," Prin said.

"I know that! I love my granddaughters! It's not about them, son," Kingsley said.

"Then what, Dad? Really? You know, you must know, the chances of my having another child are—"

"Don't say it," Kingsley said.

But there was no command in his voice, only cracking. Kingsley's nose tingled like someone had just smashed it with a mango. But damn them, he never cried when they'd smash his nose on all those walks home from school in a Colombo laneway. When he wouldn't cry at the smashed nose, the older boys would make him walk past the canteen where his mother worked.

The first chance he had, Kingsley applied to leave it all behind and start again.

Clean slate.

White as snow.

Canada.

And you don't build a life like this, you don't keep it going, by dwelling and dwelling on why your wife left you or why she then married a terroristic grocer or how it could be that the man lying in a hospital bed is still, is always, your child, your little boy on the bench of the Caprice, or how it could be that something has been taken out of him that could have killed him. Damned cancer!

But it was gone, and now what mattered was what happened next, what needed to happen next, to keep it all going and going and going.

"Fine. If you can't, then I will," Kingsley said.

"You will what?" Prin said.

But Kingsley had already gone into the corridor to call everyone else back into the hospital room. The girls crowded around the bed. Lizzie pulled out her bag of rosaries. Parking was by the hour, so Kingsley invited Kareem to offer a prayer of thanks for Prin's successful operation, which confused and quieted Lizzie and her beads. Kareem demurred until Kingsley commanded him to recite. Then, after Kareem's longish prayer to a sort-of-every-God, Kingsley asked Molly if she and the girls wanted to visit a martyr's shrine north of the city for some real prayers… and candy! The girls cheered.

7

A FEW WEEKS later, on Mardi Gras, Kingsley dropped Molly and the girls at the martyr's shrine. He handed out bags of leftover Halloween candy.

Promise kept!

Molly tried to say—but father and son were already driving away.

Prin didn't complain as much as he might have. Just as everyone was getting out of Kingsley's already moving car, he had seen Fr. Pat, the president of his university, step down from a luxury motor coach and lead a group of white-haired women and men with canes and walkers into the same shrine. Seeing Prin out here, like this, upright and moving about with only mild discomfort, Fr. Pat might have asked him if he wanted to return to work earlier than planned.

Prin didn't want to go back just yet. He was very much enjoying his time at home. He made breakfast, he walked the kids to and from the bus, and otherwise puttered around, reading, napping, praying, doing some simple stretching exercises, sorting the mail and salting the sidewalks, deleting, unread, every message from work, and in all this he gloried in thinking and thinking about what he was going to do with this new life, and in feeling pretty much like he was already doing exactly what God desired that he do. Because now and then, Jesus must have puttered. And meanwhile, of her own silent accord, thanks be to God, Molly had changed her sleeping position.

Feeling so contentedly Christ-like, Prin had been looking forward to offering a prayer of thanksgiving at the martyr's shrine where centuries before, missionaries had founded a church upon the spot where, by pious tradition, a little Indian girl had seen a vision of the Virgin that turned her brown eyes blue. But his father had other plans. As Prin and Kingsley pulled into the parking lot of a giant metal barn, Prin pictured Molly and the girls there in the church, kneeling before the image of a blue-green Mother Mary floating among the cedar trees and, above them, with them, dangling from the rafters, dozens of cobwebbed crutches slowly turning in the small breezes that came every time a pilgrim opened the great doors.

"So, just to check, when he says 'No more bets, gentlemen,' what do you do?" Kingsley asked.

"Sorry, what was that, Dad?" Prin said.

"Did you get hearing cancer, too? This whole time, I've been telling you how we're going to bet at the roulette tables. When he says 'No more bets, gentlemen,' you throw down ten chips!" Kingsley said.

"I like that we're spending time together like this, Dad, but—"

"We're not *spending time together*. Whether you have your prostate or not, don't talk like a woman, Prin. We're here because you survived and we're going to celebrate by winning enough money to pay for our flights to Sri Lanka," Kingsley said.

"Dad, about that. Were you really serious, in the hospital, about planning to remarry?" Prin asked.

"You must have been confused by the medications," Kingsley said.

"So that means—" Prin said.

"Why is that priest looking funny at you?" Kingsley asked.

Prin looked over. It was Fr. Pat again, standing in the middle of that same sea of white-haired people, only now they were all struggling to pull on plastic green poker visors and bright, beaded necklaces. Before Prin could duck and tie his shoe, the two men made eye contact. But then Fr. Pat knelt down to tie his own shoe.

Why would his boss be avoiding a conversation with him? Did he know some terrible news, like Prin's committee assignments for when he returned?

Prin told Kingsley he'd meet him at the roulette tables ("TABLE FOUR! THE ONE WITH THE DEALER WHO SMILES LIKE HE DOESN'T SPEAK ENGLISH. LOOK FOR THE SHORT, FAT ARMS.") and made his way across the dim, dinging, crowded space. Fr. Pat got up just as he reached him. He was well into his seventies, like many of Prin's colleagues at the university.

"Oh Prin, how good to see you upright and among the living and the gambling!" Fr. Pat said.

"You too, Father Pat. And thank you for that note you sent when I was in the hospital," Prin said.

"But tell me, was it better than Sister Contra Melanchthon's famous shortbread? I hear you got a tin!" Fr. Pat said.

The priest tittered, waiting for Prin either to join him or leave. This was also his basic approach to governing the university. Prin smiled but stayed put. He needed to know why Fr. Pat had tried to duck him. Was he going to be assigned to the Inter-Departmental Curriculum Review Committee, again?

"So how's campus these days?" Prin asked.

"Never mind that! How are you feeling? How goes the recovery? Good enough to gamble, I see!" Fr. Pat said.

"My Dad brought me with him. Actually, we were at the shrine earlier," Prin said.

"I thought I saw your beautiful family there!" Fr. Pat said.

But then the priest's toothy smile vanished. He dropped down to tie his other shoe. He was down there a long time. Prin finally dropped down to one knee as well.

Fr. Pat was wearing Velcro!

"Father Pat, is there something happening on campus? Can I help?" Prin asked.

"I'm afraid we all need to help, Prin. We all need some help," he said.

Now, instead of tittering, he squinted his eyes and nodded slowly.

"Sorry, Father Pat, but could you be a little more specific?" Prin asked.

"I see. So you haven't been reading my Metaphysical Therapist blog," said Fr. Pat.

Prin checked his own shoes.

"Attention, Class of '68!" one of the endless old ladies around them said. "Father Pat is waiting for us to join him in the rosary before we hit the tables."

At that, dozens of titanium knees sprang and hinged into action. Groaning and supplications to Mary followed.

"Prin, can you hear me?" Fr. Pat asked.

"Yes, Father," Prin said.

"Did you ever hear the one about the fat man who went to confession?" Fr. Pat asked.

"No," Prin said.

"He says 'Bless me Father, I have sinned.' But he's so fat, it comes out as 'Bless me Father, I have thinned.' And the priest peeks through the grate and says, 'Not enough!'"

Prin waited. Fr. Pat stopped tittering and sighed.

"Okay, so jokes aside, our school is in a bit of trouble," Fr. Pat said.

"Unless I join the Inter-Departmental Review Committee, again, right?" Prin said.

"No, not like that. But thank you for volunteering. I will let the dean know you are happy to serve—"

"Actually I'm not, Father Pat," Prin said.

"It doesn't matter," Fr. Pat said.

"Of course it does! Academic freedom!" Prin said.

The priest said something under his breath. Prin couldn't hear it for all the Hail Marys around them.

"I didn't catch that, Father," Prin said.

"Listen, son. For years and years I've been warning all of you about this, and now it's true. We are facing a grave problem with our budget," Fr. Pat said.

"What is it? Are you going to try to cut the interlibrary-loan service again?" Prin asked.

This was often the source of the Armageddon that took place at the annual spring all-faculty meeting.

"We're almost out of money," Fr. Pat said.

"So why don't you just fundraise more?" Prin said.

"You have small children, right Prin?" Fr. Pat asked.

"Yes. Why?" Prin asked.

"Never mind. The university will close down at the end of this year unless we find a new source of funding. And no, son, the answer is not just more fundraising. There's going to be a special all-faculty meeting in a couple of weeks. You should be there," Fr. Pat said.

"Okay…" Prin said.

"And in the mean time, win big!" Fr. Pat said, standing back up, his big bright Irish grin nearly back in place as he roused his rosary circle to make for the slots.

Prin joined his father at the roulette table and mechanically followed his commands. They were up, they were down, they were really up, and then they were really, really, really up, and then they were banned from the table for ignoring the "Last Bets" rule one too many times. His plan working perfectly, Kingsley scooped up their winnings and made his way to another table staffed by another tubby, goateed dealer and they did it all again. This time a manager was called to warn Kingsley that one more infraction and he'd be banned from the casino for a month. Again.

"So, are we splitting the winnings?" Prin asked.

"Of course! Minus my staking you, and the cost of the flights, we split the winnings," Kingsley said.

"Dad, I might need more than that," Prin said.

"Why? What's wrong? You're cured. What's wrong?" said Kingsley.

He couldn't do it. Just then his father's sharp brow and hard eyes went soft and slack and he was a worried old man standing in the middle of a big, dark barn, his hands fretting. The only thing—the *only* thing—Prin's father understood about his becoming a professor was that it was a lifetime job. Molly understood more than that, if not why Prin was so passionately convinced that descriptions of marine creatures were fundamental to the meaning of modern Canadian literature. But she too, finally, abided all of the small, dramatic outrages that Prin brought home from work because, unlike her own, late father, who only ever came home from work grimy and looking for a cold beer, Prin would never be transferred, or laid off, or informed by a smiling twenty-five-year-old girl in funeral black that he'd been made redundant.

And yet Prin had just been informed that his entire university, a school that had existed for more than a century, might soon be redundant. His life was spared so he could lose his job? Their house? What kind of God did that to a man? What kind of work could he get? He was forty years old and trained to identify the little sea creatures swimming around in Canadian prairie poetry. What kind of work did God expect him to get?

But nothing was certain, yet. In addition to the all-faculty meeting that had been called to discuss the situation, Fr. Pat told him a consultant had been hired. He had said Prin shouldn't worry yet, or worry his family yet, either.

"PRIN! I asked you, what's wrong?" Kingsley said.

"I was just thinking it'd be nice to bring Molly along if we go to Sri Lanka," Prin said.

Kingsley's hands became fists. He punched his son on both shoulders. Chips fell out of his bulging pockets. "That's my boy! If the cure works, why waste time?" Kingsley said. "Now pick up those chips and let's go win your wife the trip of her lifetime!"

They lost everything at the next table.

8

THE ALL-FACULTY MEETING took place in a dark octagonal room covered in bright, bold signs.

BLESS UFU

WE ARE UFU

I LOVE UFU

GO UFU

GOD BLESS UFU

PARENT OF UFU

PARENTAL FIGURE OF UFU

UFU STANDS FOR UFU

Prin worked at a school that had been founded in Toronto in the middle of the nineteenth century by an order of Irish priests from Boston, one of whom was said to have heard John F. Kennedy's lone confession while president. The priest died shortly thereafter. The school was originally called Holy Family College. By the middle of the twentieth century it was doing well enough to become the University of the Holy Family.

Professors and alumni eventually expressed concern that the school was becoming increasingly irrelevant and too Catholic-seeming, so they changed its name to the University of the Family Universal and went by U.F.U. In turn, members of the business school pointed out the challenge of explaining the acronym. Now the school was simply UFU. It stood for UFU.

It also had an app.

In spite of all of this, the school was still in grave trouble. After hearing the news from Fr. Pat at the casino, Prin had read his blog that night and two weeks later—in slushy, bar-ren-branched mid-March Toronto—he interrupted his medical leave to attend a meeting with his fellow professors. That morning, he'd told Molly he needed a book from his office. They hugged and kissed as brother and sister, and he left for campus.

Prin took a seat at a plastic board-room table in the middle of an octagonal room that had once been a mediaeval manuscript library and was now *The Charles "Chipper" Sullivan and Family Memorial Multifunction Bookable Function Room 1b*. Its peeling beige walls were pockmarked and shaded oaken brown in the outline of the bookcases that had once lined them. They were now covered in posters from the university's latest marketing campaign.

Why was everyone in such good spirits? The platters of cheesecake bites could only explain so much. His being there explained even less. His colleagues were glad to see him but Prin wasn't an especially prominent member of the faculty.

Despite a series of well-received regional emerging scholars' association-sponsored conference presentations on the penis shaped like a sleeping seahorse that figures prominently in Michael Ondaatje's *The English Patient*, Prin had yet to publish any major work on marine life in the Canadian literary landscape, but he taught assorted survey classes and accepted committee assignments without much complaint. Also, he had agreed to be the faculty advisor to the university's Catholic students' club, comprised of six Chinese communications majors who spoke little English. The occasional seventh member was a mature Filipino student who smiled a lot and cried uncontrollably whenever when she saw Prin's daughters. She was on a scholarship that might have been connected to her working, years before, as a nanny for the university's chief fundraiser.

"If I may call us to attention," Fr. Pat said.

He then invited the oldest member of the faculty, an emeritus classics professor, to lead the group in an opening prayer. A priest pushed a walker up to the podium that had been set up at one end of the room, in the middle of the U-shaped table. A pierced and tattooed AV attendant adjusted the microphone radically down.

The old man smiled at everyone, whirred back at Fr. Pat to confirm he should start, and then took off his Red Sox cap and offered a wedding blessing in Biblical Greek.

"Thank you, Fr. O'Shaughnessy," said Fr. Pat.

He waited for the old man to return to the corner of the table, where with some panache he twirled his walker around and sat down on its built-in bench. Everyone clapped, as usual; also as usual there was already someone standing behind him to stop his walker from careening backwards into the wall. The priest was pushed back to the table and nodded at the president, who smiled, sighed, and began.

"Friends, I have called this meeting so that, as a community, we can discuss the grave challenge before our beloved institution," said Fr. Pat.

The room became very still. Prin looked around. The professors were sour-faced and whispering back and forth. None of them had read the blog! But then a hand shot up. It belonged to the leader of the faculty association, a bearded, denim-clad labour historian.

"Yes, Professor Bergermaster, I thought I'd hear from you, first," said Fr. Pat.

"Listen, Father Pat, we work in a spirit of transparency and openness and collaboration. That said, if you think the university can get away with this, you're very wrong," said Professor Bergermaster.

"I'm sorry, Breen, but the Board Finance Committee has studied the situation extensively, and it is dire," said Fr. Pat.

"But you say this every year! And every year, in the end, you figure out a way to pay for the interlibrary-loan service," said Professor Bergermaster, to angry ayes.

Fr. Pat reached forward a little on the podium, his hands gripping its front and slipping. The university's old crest—Jesus, Mary, and Joseph living in a house made of books—had been pried off long before. In its place was a bare, bright space.

"This has nothing to do with funding for the interlibrary-loan program," Fr. Pat said.

The room filled with sighs of relief.

"None of you read his blog!" said Prin.

Everyone looked down at their cheesecake crumbs. The younger professors began searching for the blog on their phones. The older faculty tried to figure out the Wi-Fi.

"We are glad to see you again, Prin," Fr. Pat said. "I'm only sorry we can't welcome you back on happier terms. But if Prin is correct, then, my friends, I am even more disappointed. As you all know, for months now *The Metaphysical Therapist* has been my forward-looking way of engaging our community. It's even available on our app, iTouchUFU. But if even the faculty of this university can't be troubled to read it, then maybe we shouldn't be surprised at our broader situation.

"Anyway, perhaps take a moment to read my latest post, and then, as a community committed to comity and unity and forging a way forward that is inclusive of everyone, we can reflect—"

"WHAT THE HELL IS THIS?"

Thirty minutes later, the meeting was called back to order. Other people had by now entered the room—a squat Chinese man with spiky hair and two phones going at once, and a tall, funereal-looking Arab man in a dark suit. In a back corner, studying documents, stood a third, a thin blonde woman in leather boots and metallic jewellery.

"Friends, let's try again," Fr. Pat said.

Sixty minutes later, he tried again. By this point, all the professors had had a chance to say something. None were interested in learning more about falling enrolments and rising pension costs, or about how fundraising fell apart after the head of the capital campaign, Seamus Michael O'Gorman, Class of '66, made a joke about drag racing his Trans Am at a young alumni mixer.

They showed no sympathy about the latest pair of lawsuits the university was forced to settle related to a gender-rights case connected to its annual biathlon, and to its having invited students to read a novel by a young Indigenous author about corruption-fighting vampires who were Indigenous youth leaders. Following a dramatic online investigation, the novel turned out to have been written by a middle-aged Indigenous author.

Prin felt bad for Fr. Pat, who was turning tomato-red under his shock of white hair while the professors had at him. Prin didn't join in, but he didn't defend the president, either. If UFU was really going to close in a year, he was in the same situation as his colleagues. Many of them still had mortgages and children living at home. Beneath those prosperous, busy heavens, Toronto had a lot of crowded, dry ground.

"Maybe if we stopped with all the catered cheesecake, that would help. I mean, what are we, Minnesota Lutherans? You all know I'd happily bake shortbread for meetings," said Sister Contra Melanchthon.

"Maybe we need a new website?" a professor asked.

"Or 3D printers? Aren't they ... something ... now?" another professor asked.

"What about tuition? Can't we raise it?" still another professor asked.

"We just don't have enough students these days, as you all know," Fr. Pat said.

"But we have some! And we owe it to them to keep this place open!" another professor said.

This sounded good. Everyone cared about the students and demanded the school stay open—for them, the students. Fr. Pat let them go on for a while and then pointed out that the students were all eligible to transfer to other schools and would do so without much trouble and, he lamented, without much complaint.

"Well, I thought the whole point of your selling all the buildings except this one was to pay for that kind of stuff! Can't you just sell this one too, and pay us to teach online?" another of Prin's colleagues asked.

"It's funny you should say that," Fr. Pat said. "As you all know from reading my entire blog post concerning this matter"—again everyone looked down, scrolling furiously, Prin included—"and specifically after I quote at length from the Pope's recent reflections on—"

"PLEASE JUST TELL US YOU HAVE A PLAN TO SAVE OUR JOBS!"

"He doesn't, and that's why he hired me," said the woman standing in the shadows behind Fr. Pat.

He gratefully gave way as she took over the podium.

"Hello everyone. My name is Wende. Hello, Prin."

He almost snapped his pencil.

9

HIS EX-GIRLFRIEND FROM graduate school told his colleagues her story, mentioning her connection to Prin only in passing—that they had gone to school together many years before. Everyone was so worried, she could have told them she and Prin used to run a factory where African orphans made earmuffs out of baby seals and they would still have asked her to get to the point. What was her plan to save UFU? And how had she remained this thin, for this long?

Prin couldn't see a wedding ring. But yes, what was her plan to save UFU?

"I created my company after my job at a college in Montana was eliminated a few months ago. Believe me, I tried and tried to find another position. I even thought about teaching high school..."

They gasped.

"But then I decided that what I went through should never have to happen to another professor. Today I specialize in identifying financially viable options for under-performing academic institutions to continue delivering content," Wende said.

Many hands went up.

"To answer the first question I get, every time: my approach ensures that all current staff continue on in their positions, at their current salaries," Wende said.

All the hands went down. Then all the hands went up again.

"To answer the second question, it doesn't necessarily have to involve teaching in the summer," Wende said.

All the hands went down.

"So, in the case of UFU, I have identified two options that I think are worth exploring. With me today are representatives from two institutions interested in creating partnerships with your school that would allow it to stay open. Father Pat invited us here today to explain these opportunities. The plan would be for committees to be struck to consider each opportunity and present recommendations to the president and the board before September. I will offer my consulting services to both committees, and serve as liaison with our prospective partner institutions. How's all of this sound, out of curiosity?" said Wende.

No one said anything. Beards were furiously scratched. A stream of swear words in Biblical Greek cut through the silence.

"Then with your permission, perhaps it'd be best to hear directly from our prospective suitors," said Wende.

She stepped away from the podium and smiled at everyone, including Prin. The stocky Chinese man took over. He explained he was the CEO of a building company that specialized in "wraparound lifestyle for the golden years." He proposed purchasing and then converting UFU's last remaining building into Toronto's best elder-care assisted-living facility, with the professors staying on to offer "fun," "stress-free" classes and workshops to residents.

The Arab man spoke next. He told the faculty he was actually an alumnus of UFU from the late 1970s who, after a successful career in business in New York, had returned to his native Dragomans to accept a position as a cabinet minister with the transitional government that had been formed after the end of its civil war, "the brutalities of which, I needn't tell you about, I am sure," he said.

Everyone murmured sympathetically in the hopes there wouldn't be a pop quiz about Dragomans' civil war, or about Dragomans itself.

The Minister proceeded into a long and—if you weren't worried about losing your job—moving story about visiting refugee camps around the country, and about meeting one young woman in particular, Mariam. She'd grown up in a Dragomans village, where people of different faiths had lived together in harmony for centuries. Once the extremists arrived, however, the village was destroyed, and Mariam and her family, who were not Muslim but part of an older religion, had gone into hiding in the mountains behind their burned-down home. They were found. Her brothers and father were taken in one truck. Her mother and sisters were taken in another. She never saw any of them again. She was the oldest daughter and was promised to one of the fighters. He traded her to another man for engine parts. That man was kind and left her at a refugee camp, which is where the Minister found her.

"I asked her what she wanted to do with her life, now that peace had returned to our land. She told me her father always wanted her brothers to become engineers and so, because she had been spared, she wanted to be an engineer too, for all of them, and, my friends, for the glorious future of our beloved Dragomans!"

The Minister waited in vain for applause. Finally, after much heated debate amongst a group of professors, the leader of the faculty association raised his hand.

"Thank you. That's very moving. We hope you succeed. But, well, sorry, but, well, what's this have to do with us?" asked Professor Bergermaster.

"Everything!" the Minister said.

Still no damned applause.

Wende returned to the podium and explained that the government of Dragomans was interested in opening a new university but at present it had no professors. Hands went up and she said there would be no faculty transfers. Hands went down. Instead, this proposed new university was in need of a school in North America that, in exchange for generous, long-term funding, would offer online teaching and grant degrees to its students, and also, when security conditions allowed for it, send one faculty member a month to offer an in-person lecture. Wende said she'd accompany the first faculty member.

Prin was sure she looked at him when she said this.

10

AFTER MUCH MORE furious beard-scratching and Greco-Biblical imprecating and impassioned invocations of assorted codicils to various university-governance documents, the professors grumbled their agreement with the plan.

"And now, to ensure the integrity of this work, we require representation from the faculty," Fr. Pat said. "I know everyone already does so much, but please, consider volunteering for this. All our futures depend on it."

"I agree, but I'm already doing curriculum committee."

"I agree, but I'm already doing grade appeals and academic integrity."

"I'm doing the review of the Senate minutes review protocol draft."

"Well, I'm doing high school and community outreach."

"I'm doing the young alumni."

"I'm doing students with mental-health challenges."

"I'm doing students with disabilities."

"I'm doing international students AND I'm doing the friends of the library."

"I thought I was doing the friends of the library."

"There's so many, we can do them together if that sounds fun."

It appeared that every faculty member was already doing something, or someone, on behalf of UFU, except Prin. He agreed to return to work early and to do the Chinese property developer and also do the Dragomans Minister. Wende would help.

The meeting was adjourned. Fr. Pat introduced the Chinese developer and the Dragomans Minister to the slower-moving professors and to Sister Contra Melanchthon's shortbread while Wende walked across the room to greet Prin. She cocked her head and wrinkled her eyes and smiled expectantly. Had she smiled that way, years before? He didn't remember. He couldn't, or at least, he wouldn't. He got up, eased around the table, and they hugged like brother and sister porcupines.

"So, Prin, it's been a long time," she said.

"Indeed. I'm sorry your situation in Montana didn't work out," he said.

"Don't be. It was a terrible job in the middle of nowhere. But this new work is endless, I'm making a lot more money and travelling all over the place. I'm single, still, and don't even have a cat. I wouldn't mind one, but that's one cliché too many, right?" she said.

"Your resistance to cliché continues, I see," he said.

"As does your very careful wording when you're nervous. But why are you nervous now?" she asked.

"I'm not," he said.

She leaned in and her teeth flashed in a sudden smile.

"I've asked you that question before. Remember?" she asked.

"No. Would you like some shortbread?" he said.

"That conversation we had, after … Don't you remember?" she asked.

"No," he said.

This was no lie. He only remembered it after she asked him. He started saying Hail Mollys to forget. Hail Marys.

"Okay, Prin. You don't want to play. That's fine. But look, unfortunately for UFU its situation has brought me here, but I'm glad to see you again," she said.

"Would you like to see a picture of my wife and kids?" he asked.

He held his phone in front of him like the very shield of heaven. She studied the image of Molly and the girls beaming and giggling on a ferry bench, going across to the Toronto Islands the summer before.

"Same old Abelard. The worrying little Catholic boy. I think you can say you're glad to see me too and not lose what you think of as your soul. And because of this project with UFU, you'll be seeing more of me," she said.

Wende was still smiling, but a little sourly, or at least she might have been wearing sour apple lip-balm, he thought. She used to. It left a sharp, sweet taste on your lips.

Wende kissed him lightly on both cheeks before he could step back. Then she gathered her things and walked out of the room, firm and full in her slim black pants. He looked and looked away, his soul full of sour apples.

11

AFTER THE FACULTY meeting, Prin walked past the subway and into an old city church. It was far enough away from campus that none of the priests from UFU would be there. Its copper was long gone green, its stone spires soared with help from red steel posts, and its alabaster angels and supplicant saints had been host to generations of pigeons but still they stood, still they smiled and beckoned.

The church was hemmed in on one side by an even older-looking small-motor repair shop, and on the other by a bar and magic-supply store called Swizzle Styx. He had come in only to take a moment before the altar, to kneel and think and pray and wait for a small tremble, for some kind of answer.

What have I done, Lord?

He had looked as she'd walked away, yes, but he had looked away. But then he did not take his moment before the altar. When he saw, in the dim back corner beside the tray of guttering votives to St Jude, that the little red light was on in front of the confessional, he went there instead. The span of one old lady's shriving wasn't long enough to let him decide what it was, but there was something he needed to tell. It was something. Wasn't it? He ducked in through burgundy velvet curtains and knelt down.

"Bless me, Father, for I have sinned. Maybe. At least, I think so," Prin said.

"Well. This is interesting," the priest said.

"I'm not trying to be interesting," Prin said.

"You've come to confession but you're not sure you have anything to confess. I've been sitting here for three hours, first with the executive committee of the parish women's council and then with the grade-three class of Pope Francis Elementary. It's been all hardness of heart towards daughters-in-law who make boxed cakes and kids putting plastic in the compost bin on purpose. Like being stoned to death with popcorn. You're not sure if you've sinned, which suggests to me you've done something that makes your heart restless. So tell me, is your heart restless?" the priest said.

"Well, Father, I signed up for a certain committee at work," Prin said.

The priest sighed.

"You must be from the university," the priest said.

"I am, and yes, perhaps I can speak more clearly, in light of your somehow sensing that I'm a professor," Prin said.

"I can certainly sense that. Alright then. Please continue," the priest said.

More popcorn.

"And do you mind if I put it in my own language?" Prin asked.

"I'm sure I've heard worse, my son," the priest said.

"Okay. Well, part of the matter troubling me, Father, concerns the counterposing imperatives of my personal and professional vocations, the feeling that fulfilling one might undermine the other—"

"So you work too much and you think you should be at home more but then you can't provide as much or as well. And the sin is?" the priest asked.

"No, Father, it's more that any reasonable interrogation of the interior movements that informed my agreeing to serve on a particular committee in light of the external representative on the same committee—"

"Do you hear that? What's it sound like?" the priest asked.

Prin listened to the sound. It was small and insistent. The youngest child in a family of sounds.

"It sounds like…"

"It sounds like me tapping a key on my watch, yes?" the priest said.

"Oh. Yes, right. I'm sorry for taking so long. There's no one else waiting, as far as I know, but I appreciate you might want to go. Sorry, Father," Prin said.

"No! Don't apologize. I'll be here all night with you if need be. But you're enjoying your professorizing too much. I've certainly heard worse language in here, but not by much. Let's clear it away. Let me help you with that. Listen again. What's that sound like?" the priest said.

Tock   tock   tock

Prin suddenly wanted just a fast absolution and some Hail Marys. But at least this priest was trying to help him name his sin, if sin it be. Had the priest been younger and more Filipino, like Prin's usual confessors in the city, he would have told Prin that Jesus loved him no matter what, then giggled, then told him that for his absolution he should call his mother every day for a month. Then giggled.

"What else?" the priest asked again, still tappping.

Tock   tock   tock

"It's constant, um, and sounds like, well yes, a key on a watchface. But also, perhaps, like someone checking the ice before walking on it?" Prin said.

Tock   tock   tock

"Or … someone tapping on a window … is it supposed to be God tapping on the window of my soul?" Prin asked.

"It sounds, from far off, as far off as you might be right now, like someone hammering nails into a man's hands and feet," the priest said.

"Oh," Prin said.

"And the sound's coming from far away, and it's going on and on, and you're sitting here, far away, wasting all that time He spent like that, like this, for you. Talking and talking because you're afraid to say anything real. Now, what did you do? What did you do, to Him?" the priest asked.

Prin wanted him to stop tapping. He wanted to leave the confessional and go home and hug Molly and email Fr. Pat that he'd rather lose his job than serve on a committee where he'd have to spend time with Wende.

But wait. What did it matter? Even if he wanted to, and he did not want to, he just didn't want to be in a situation where he might want to, but even if that happened, he couldn't do anything.

He really, actually, technically, couldn't.

Was his diminishment part of God's plan for him, for all of them? Did he get prostate cancer so he could chastely work closely with his ex-girlfriend and save his job and his family while also helping a Middle Eastern orphaned Christian girl go to school?

Was this the twenty-first century saint's life that God had suddenly made possible for him?

Prin had all of this in his heart but, in truth, while she remained lithe and firm after all these years, he hadn't felt anything when he saw Wende or when they had hugged or when she had pecked his cheeks or even when he had thought about that lip-balm. He thought about it again, just then, in the confessional.

Nothing!

He actually didn't care if she still wore it. Because in none of this had he *felt* felt, even when he had looked at her walking away and then looked away. And even if she'd also looked at him, and she had, for a moment, she definitely had... what did it matter? People look at each other all the time. He'd just been worried he might have *felt* felt. But he hadn't. He didn't. And he couldn't. And he never would. He could tell all of this.

He could go home and tell Molly all of this. Tell, not confess.

Because he had Molly! He had been granted Molly, who didn't visit innovative business solutions upon the poor professors of failing universities. Who had always said far more than merely *Whatever you think is best, dear*. It was only his hard heart, his hearing that had made her out that way. Well, she did say it sometimes, sometimes a lot, but she was far more than that. In fact, seeing Wende today, Wende's life as it was, today, helped him to this.

Where was the sin in such discovery?

There was no sin, only gratitude!

"Thank you, Father. I think you've helped me understand my situation. I apologize for taking up your time like this, but I actually have nothing to confess," Prin said.

"Really? You're sure? In the twenty years I've been tapping my watch in the confessional, you're the first person to hear it and not confess anything," the priest said.

"Well of course, of course I have some sins. What about, so, let's see, yes, a lack of charity towards my loved ones, and also vanity and pride. Also, sometimes... when praying the Our Father, of saying 'Our Father, who art in heaven, Han Solo be thy name'" Prin said.

"I like the old Star Wars movies. The new ones feel like toy commercials set to Wagner. But those are your same-old sins, son. They can't be what brought you in here. Has whatever it was truly passed?" the priest asked.

"Yes," Prin said.

"Very well. You know your mind, your heart. As does God. If whatever it was returns, you know where to find me. My name's Father Tom, and I'm usually here because I'm usually the only one here, the only one left. For your penance, say five Our Fathers—proper Our Fathers—and now make an act of contrition."

12

MOLLY MET HIM at the door in sweatpants. He hugged her with a force fit to shatter a porcupine. She laughed and hugged him back. But she couldn't pull away. Prin held her so long that the children left their crafts and colouring books and crowded into the threshold. They tugged on their parents' legs and pushed on their elbows, trying either to join the hug or figure out why Daddy was hugging Mommy for so long. Molly was wondering the same. Every follow-up appointment since his surgery had been fine.

Had someone called from the doctor's office?

Was there news?

"Prin, is everything okay?" she asked.

"I'm happy to see you, to see all of you!" he said.

He proposed skipping the Instant Pot for a night and going out for brick-oven pizza, to cheers all around, and picked up around the house while Molly changed. When they got back from the restaurant, he insisted on putting the kids to bed on his own while Molly had a glass of wine in the living room.

"Prin, now I'm really wondering what's going on," she said.

He joined her on the couch, smiling and studying her big blue eyes, the forever rose in her cheeks. She wasn't slim, she was gaunt. She wasn't sleek, she was cold, whereas Molly was warm and full and waiting to find out what they were celebrating.

"Like I said, I'm happy to see you, to see all of you," he said.

And he didn't even mean it that way! Or rather he did, he was happy to see *all* of her. He remembered hugging Wende. Then, as now, it was crinkly and poky, like carrying a bundle of brush.

"Prin, there's something you need to tell me. What is it? Are you feeling sick? Did the doctor call? Did something happen at work?" Molly asked.

"I'm not feeling sick and the doctor didn't call but yes, something happened at work, and it's not great news," Prin said.

"Bad committee work again?" she asked.

"Actually, sort of, yes," Prin said.

And so Prin told her everything. At least, he told her everything that made sense to tell, at that point, in the sacramentally valid context of having had his lack of charity towards her forgiven a few hours earlier. Molly was worried by the news of UFU's potential closing and didn't know what to think about the options for keeping it going. She knew exactly what to think, however, when she found out about Prin's having to work with Wende. She put her glass down on the coffee table so hard it toppled a nearby Lego crucifix.

"So this is all guilt. The hug, the pizza, the picking up around the house, the wine, the commitment to helping Middle Eastern Christian orphans. All guilt. But what really upsets me is that you feel like there's something to be guilty about. You mentioned this woman back when we first started dating, but you didn't make it out to be a big thing," she said.

"Because it wasn't! Molly, it's not that at all," Prin said.

He waited, thinking she'd start crying, but she didn't. Instead, she looked out their front window. He didn't know what to say next either so he got down on his knees and began to piece back together the Lego crucifix. He gave Jesus a helmet of hard brown plastic hair and wondered if it would help to remind her why, post-operatively, he really had nothing to be guilty about, even if he wanted to be. But that could lead to a whole other set of speculations. And there was no need. He had *felt* felt nothing! The littlest red pieces, rose heads, plastic stigmata, fit into place in silence. No tapping. He was that close now. Was he that close now? *Lord, am I that close?*

The bearded, yellow-faced Lego Jesus smiled at him but gave up no ghost.

Molly stood up and said she understood he needed to be part of this committee to save the university, and that it wasn't his fault his ex-girlfriend was involved. She only wanted to make sure it wasn't Prin who had contacted her. He nearly pointed out that he hadn't Googled her in ages, certainly not in months. Why had he been Googling in the first place? Never mind. We all do, right? His browser history had also long since been shriven.

"Molly, what can I do to assure you there's nothing to worry about?" he asked.

"Whatever you think is best, dear," Molly said.

With a bit of a bite.

One of the girls called Molly from upstairs. Prin offered to go. Molly ignored him and went, then called him to come quickly. He dashed up the stairs ready to do everything he could to show his love for her, for them, and reached the room just as Philomena began throwing up in her bed.

They continued arguing about Wende the next night while washing and folding laundry. Meanwhile, Fr. Pat had asked Prin to begin his committee work by scheduling a Skype meeting with representatives from the school in Dragomans, and also to give a talk on later-life learning to a seniors' group who might be potential residents of a future condo on the university's grounds. It would be five more nights of washing and folding laundry before Prin and Molly could finish their own conversation—after Philomena came Chiara, then Maisie, then Pippa, on Molly, and finally Prin. It was either stomach flu or food poisoning from bad pizza.

"I guess there's one thing you can do, Prin, to make me feel better about this," Molly said.

"Name it," Prin said.

"Invite her over for dinner," Molly said.

13

WENDE DIDN'T COME alone. She also didn't bring a date. At least Prin presumed she had not brought a date.

"I'm Rae," said a short, business-dressed Chinese woman.

Molly was still in the kitchen when the two of them pulled up in a Lexus. Their daughters—scrubbed, combed, and arranged oldest to youngest in pretty dresses—awaited the guests just inside the front door.

"You have a big shiny car for just two people!" said Chiara.

"Thank you. And you all look beautiful. You have a very charming home," said Wende.

How small their house was. It was a ninety-year-old semi-detached with three bedrooms and a half-finished basement located at the top of a hill in the city's east end. Looking south on clear winter days, you could see straight across Lake Ontario to the smoke and crumbling block of Buffalo.

The house itself had been renovated many times over the years, but never fully or especially well, which is why they had been able to afford it. The result was exposed brick here and there; hollow, fake-panelled doors set in original gumwood frames; thick, well-scored old oak floors running into click-in-place artificial oak whose surface was a reasonable facsimile of thick, well-scored old oak floors, at least where it wasn't peeling. The bathroom looked like the Before shot in a home renovation show. Their furniture wasn't all shabby and certainly not all chic, but a combination of interesting yard-sale finds, better IKEA, and random pieces of fine, nineteenth-century German craftsmanship—end tables and side chairs and such, all the colour of blackstrap molasses—which they'd brought home from Molly's grandmother's Milwaukee bungalow over the years.

The walls were mostly—but not entirely!—covered in religious art and family photographs. Prin's mother frequently gave Molly silver-plated trays from Sri Lanka meant for hanging, not serving, that featured images of monks, elephants, and monkeys, and ceremonial processions of monks, elephants, and monkeys. These were propped up in advance of Lizzie's visits. More recently, Prin had also started propping up a Golden Rule poster, framed in a thick, filigreed oak, that Lizzie's new Muslim husband had presented to the family on his first visit to their home.

Kingsley had given them a framed picto-history series marking his life and exploits. Thanks to a clever German carpenter who also must have had a vain in-law, the pictures were affixed to the inner panel of a buffet top that could be quickly opened and prominently displayed at the sound of an impatient triple doorbell.

Prin wasn't embarrassed by any of this as he studied Wende taking in their home from the foyer. Did she notice the piles of *New Yorkers* set beside the piles of *Saint's Lives* comic books? What exactly did she notice? She'd accepted the invitation to come to dinner with no comment. But she must have been nervous, because she brought someone who, so far as Prin could tell, was not her date.

"So, how do you know Wende?" asked Prin.

"Rae's an agent," said Wende.

"ASIAN! It's pronounced ASIAN!" said Philomena.

Her sisters took her away.

"A real estate agent?" Prin asked.

"Correct," said Rae.

"Welcome!" Molly said.

She was wearing a flowing, floral-print black dress that moved with vigour as she accepted the flowers and wine and brought everyone in to their little living room. Wende wore slate-grey slacks and a white cotton dress shirt that had maybe one more button undone than was necessary.

The conversation right away focused on Rae. She had only come to Canada a few months ago, to help her uncle with his import-export business. She had left that and was now working with Wende and the developer who wanted to turn UFU into a retirement condo. Did she like Toronto? Yes. What did she like about it? It looked like a movie set for a big city and it was clean like a hospital. Did she miss home? Yes. A lot. She missed her husband and her own children. A lot. She had three daughters. Why had she come to Canada alone? Next question. Were you hoping your family would join you here? Stupid question.

"If you'll excuse me a moment, I'm going to check on the kids," Molly said.

"Why don't I?" Prin said.

"You chat with Rae. Can I offer some help, Molly?" Wende asked.

The two women walked to the kitchen together. Prin heard a buzzing, high-pitched sound. He'd never strained his ears so much! But he couldn't make out what they were saying.

"So, you're at UFU, correct?" Rae asked.

"Yes, I'm a professor there," Prin said.

"And do you pronounce the school ooo-foo, or do you say the letters like words, like You, Eff, You?"

"That's been a debate for years. People say it both ways," Prin said.

"I like You, Eff, You," Rae said.

"Me too. So, I think we'll be working together. I'm curious, what's your role in all of this?" Prin asked.

She nodded heavily, twice.

"Sorry, what's your role?" Prin asked.

"I am responsible for finding potential residents. Actually, I think we are going to do an event together, you and I, soon. Correct? That's how you say it, yes? We are going to do some old people together?" Rae said.

"Yes, I'm delivering a talk to a seniors' group. Father Pat asked me to share my research with them," Prin said.

"And if they become interested, that's great. If we can do it before that Muslim man finds you, then we get it," Rae said.

"Sorry, finds me?" Prin said.

"Students. From his country. But we will go faster and get it," Rae said.

"The contract?" Prin said.

"The contract," Rae said.

"Well, best of luck, and happy to help," Prin said.

What were they discussing in the kitchen?

"Do you mean that, really?" Rae asked.

"Pardon?" Prin said.

The children were eating early. Afterwards, they would watch another hour of *Ten Commandments* in the basement while the adults ate. Prin could hear nothing but their calls for more butterbread and less fish, less beans, and why aren't we allowed to have dessert during Lent?

"Do you really mean it, 'Best of luck and happy to help?' Canadians say things like this a lot but I don't know if you mean them. How can so many of you people really have 'No worries'?" Rae asked.

"Well, yes, I do wish you the best of luck and, as you know, my own job and those of my colleagues depend on something working out here so I am indeed happy to help," Prin said.

"So you will help me, more than you will help the Muslims?" Rae asked.

"I'm not sure I'd phrase it that way, and probably Wende should be part of this conversation, don't you think?" Prin said.

She pulled up closer to him on the couch. Prin leaned back a little, and she leaned forward.

"But she has no children. You have children. You have daughters! You understand. You must understand. *You also have daughters.* Please help me. If we get the contract, I will get enough money to bring the whole family here. Otherwise, I think he will fire me definitely, and then I will have to go back to selling kidneys. Do you know anyone who needs one?" Rae said.

"What? What are you talking about? Kidneys! Is this what your uncle's import business is about?" Prin said.

"Sorry? Must be problem with my English. So sorry, I no understand," Rae said.

She smiled a lot of teeth, sipped her wine, and stared out the front window. She kept nodding. She also kept checking to see if he was watching her. Rae said nothing more until Wende and Molly returned to the living room, at which point she got up and went into the kitchen to watch the children finish their dinner. Prin didn't know whether to stay with Wende and Molly and figure out what-kind-of-what was happening there, or to follow Rae. If he did, would he find her sobbing at these other people's daughters or sizing them for potential donations?

But instead she came back quickly, and still smiling, if with more effort. Molly invited everyone to the table, where she'd placed a pan of white beans, trout, and rosemary, beside which was a loaf of fresh-baked bread, a green salad, and the white wine that Wende had brought. They gave up alcohol during Lent. So now ought they to acknowledge the guest's gift by drinking it, or acknowledge Christ's forty days in the desert by not?

"Prin?" Molly said.

"Yes?" Prin said.

"We're waiting," Molly said.

"You want me to open the wine?" Prin asked.

"Would you like to lead us in grace?" Molly asked.

"Oh. Yes, of course. Then... wine?" Prin said.

Molly smiled.

"Whatever you think is best, dear," she said.

She smiled, but not at him. She smiled at Wende! Who was smiling back.

Just what kind of conversation did they have in the kitchen?

14

"JUST WHAT KIND of conversation did you have in the kitchen?" Prin asked after the dishes were done.

Molly smiled and said she wasn't worried about his working with Wende on a committee. Then she went upstairs to bed.

The next day, their daughters called Wende the fancy-car bone lady and Rae the real-estate Asian. Molly had had little else to say beyond reassuring Prin that Wende posed no threat. She found her nicer, and not as pretty, as she'd been expecting. And because she could tell he was going to ask something else, Molly had pointed out to Prin that it might be a good idea to spend more time on whatever he had to do through this committee to keep the university open, to keep his job, to keep them in this house, and less time wondering what his wife and long-ago ex-girlfriend had chatted about in the kitchen.

So they had chatted!

"Just what kind of conversation did you have in my kitchen? With my wife?" Prin asked when he met Wende on campus, a week later.

She said he should be more worried about the talk he was about to give. She checked her phone and went to the far side of the room, where Rae, who had set up at a folding table, was registering the old people shuffling into the UFU chapel-and-wellness space, and maybe making discreet queries about any organ-transplant needs they might have. The old people had come to campus to learn more about the condominium development and to attend Prin's lecture on Later-Life Learning about Marine Life in Canadian Literature.

He really did need to stop worrying about Molly and Wende talking. But God, even the phrase itself worried him! Not counting the girls he wrote acrostic poems for in high school—who were many, and regarded him as a wonderful friend without really appreciating the effort of the poetry, even M.A.R.Y.F.R. A.N.C.I.S.X.A.V.I.E.R. didn't!—Prin had only had one girlfriend before marrying Molly. But Wende had been, for years, no big deal beyond an occasional Google search, usually after an especially long evening of picking up baby-carrots and Lego body parts. Only now was he giving her any real thought, and that wasn't his fault. Fr. Pat had hired her. Molly had invited her to dinner. Molly had chatted and smiled with her. Molly had told him there was nothing to tell.

He arranged his notes on the lectern and surveyed the room. Decades earlier it had been a chapel. Its pews now featured thick cushions and back supports—courtesy of the Class of '52 and the Class of '57, respectively—and a series of broad, high windows overlooking the altar had been blocked off on both sides. There had once been two convent schools on the campus whose dining halls flanked the chapel. There had been legendary bun fights waged across the altar over the years, and at least one scholarly article had been published on the theological implications of a butter-roll passing over the priest's outstretched hands at the moment of consecration. The convent schools had been closed for decades, and the two dining halls were now a scent-free study space and prayer room for Muslim students.

What remained in the chapel itself were its stained-glass windows depicting scenes from the life of Christ had He had lived, died, and risen among Irish immigrants in 1920s Toronto—but it was otherwise decommissioned and used only for wellness seminars, liturgical yoga, and, as of now, academically themed real-estate presentations.

The still-great doors to the chapel suddenly banged shut, jolting everyone. The old peoples' general muttering intensified but then quieted back down when Rae distributed cookies that she announced, reading from a card, were "gluten- and allergen-free, provide twice your daily serving of vegetables, and are deliciously made according to traditional methods by a Syrian women's baking collective!"

The room was abuzz at all of this and stayed that way until Rae pulled a screen on wheels in front of the lectern and played an information video about the condominium development. Set to upbeat, nondescript music, it featured images of fit and happy old white people moving around a gleaming glass-box building built on top of a grey-stone Gothic college. The original building, in this future rendering, had been hollowed out and turned into a massive atrium lined with Apple computers and defibrillator boxes.

A soothing Asian voice, sort of male, extolled the virtues of life at The New U, where residents spent their days rolling sushi, playing pickleball, taking ballroom and hip-hop lessons, enjoying aromatherapy, learning how to code and deejay, shooting rapids and big game in virtual-reality suites, free Wi-Fi, and writing in thick leather journals embossed with REACH and DREAM and MY STORY and MY TURN and BE TODAY while bespectacled professors moved about classrooms, gesticulating and empowering inspiration. Every scene featured well-dressed groups of smiling young Arab men and women in the background, all waiting to be of assistance.

The video ended to great applause. Rae then fielded questions concerning pet policy, proximity to hospitals and to veterinary hospitals, whether walk-in tubs were standard or an upgrade, how many dog-washing stations were planned and was it first-come, first-served or by appointment, could grandchildren visits be limited to certain days and parts of the building, would there be any Indigenous values involved, was there guest parking, whether, given the affiliation of the university, the building was going to require you to be Catholic and attend Mass in order to live there, where to get more of those delicious and inspiring cookies, and then, finally, what kind of learning would take place?

"We are pleased to provide all residents of The New U building with access to highly accomplished university teachers and scholars from the Greater Toronto Area. One of these teachers is here to give you preview of the classes you can take after you buy a unit, Rae said.

Prin went to the barren-faced podium and smiled as he arranged his notes. He surveyed the white-headed crowd, wondering if he could interest them enough to want to buy a condominium. Teaching persecuted Middle-Eastern Christian millennials online might be more rewarding. His first Skype session with the staff from Dragomans was to happen the following week, a few days before Easter. As for his present audience, many were already squinting and leaning forward, even though he hadn't started lecturing yet.

When Prin noticed two dark heads bobbing at the back he also squinted, leaned forward, and yes, there it was, that unmistakable sound, one he'd known since childhood. His proud mother was shaking her many, many bangles as she waved at him. Her new Muslim husband was seated beside her, filming him with a shiny silver phone the size of an oven mitt. Why were they here? Were they planning to buy a condo? And did that mean his mother knew about the situation at UFU?

"Good afternoon ladies and gentlemen, and welcome. I am here today to propose to you that beyond the famous seahorses of Michael Ondaatje's *English Patient*, marine life more generally is an under-appreciated feature of Canadian literature, just as late-life learning is an under-appreciated feature of modern condominium living…"

After he finished, Lizzie rushed the podium, Kareem taking pictures of everything as he followed her. He braced for his mother to burst into tears but she had no idea about the circumstances of his talk. She had been simply happy, joyed, over the moon, to have seen a notice about it on her aromatherapist's Facebook. Not nearly softly enough, save for the fact that most of the people around them were basically deaf, Lizzie asked Prin how he was doing "down there," gesturing and wincing accordingly. Kareem ally-winced and continued taking pictures.

Prin said he was fine and then she asked, again very loudly, whether he had been wearing the ultra-slim premium adult diapers she'd been sending him by the case since his surgery. With unprecedented restraint, she did not check his pants. Instead, mindful she had a certain decorum to maintain as Mother of the Professor, she had Kareem squat down and study Prin for evidence. No lines! Praise God! Praise all religions! As he shifted and danced around Kareem's bobbing head, Prin saw that Wende saw.

Should he explain?

Maybe she already knew.

Did she care?

He didn't.

Did he?

He didn't.

15

ON THE MONDAY of Holy Week, Prin came to campus to have his first Skype conversation with his counterparts in Dragomans. He wasn't especially keen about this. Lecturing old people involved neither occasional travel to the Middle East nor grading, which was pretty good. He also wanted Rae to have a chance to bring her family over from China. In the days since the lecture, Prin had heard from Wende that the presentation had gone over very well, something she conveyed as much in a series of supremely businesslike notes sent through a secure messaging app called VaultTok. She told Prin that he and Rae would do more of these events between May and November, when the committee was required to make its recommendation about the future of the school. Prin had also heard directly from an older woman who attended his talk in pearls and yoga pants. She was especially taken with Prin's reflections on the seahorse-shaped penis in Michael Ondaatje's *The English Patient*. In fact, she thought the atrium should feature an aquarium filled with them (seahorses).

The UFU meeting room filled with a happy, tinny melody and the flat-screen on the far wall swirled and stuttered into the image of three light brown people sitting around a small table in a bright, bland room. They were all smiling and waving. Prin smiled and waved back. Wende was supposed to join them but she texted that she was running late, so they began the meeting without her.

Prin learned that the professors who would be working at the future UFU international campus —known as both FUFU and UFU2—were all Dragoman natives who'd been living in the US, teaching at assorted small, precarious places, and returned home to help found the new institution after the civil war ended. Some had brought their American-born children with them.

And that snowy rhinoceros at the Toronto Zoo thought *her* parents were crazy!

Wende slipped into the room just as they were discussing what kinds of connections students might make between Kafka's stories and their lives.

"It's an interesting question," Prin said.

"Is it one you could explore for us sometime?" asked Shahad, one of the fledgling Dragomans professors.

"Actually, my own area of expertise—"

"Is very much in line with that," Wende said.

"Hi Wende, good to see you again. Are we still thinking of end of July? It's the perfect time here, just when Ramadan is ending, only it'll be hotter than Montana, sorry!" said Shahad.

"Good to see you too, Shahad, and yes, that's what we're planning. It's going to be great," said Wende.

"Sorry, what's going to be great? And how do you know each other?" Prin asked.

Smiling and nodding at the screen, Wende explained that she used to work with Shahad at her old college in Montana. Just then, Fr. Pat slipped into the room and took over the conversation, making a series of jokes about his golf game, the Middle East, and sand traps. He said he was very, very grateful for their initial support. Immensely grateful. Get-down-on-both-knees grateful.

"That's not us, that's the Minister! Also, sorry, but Wende, is Prin the … Catholic one?" said Shahad.

"Yes, Prin is one of our Catholic faculty members, but like UFU itself, he is extremely inclusive and diverse," Fr. Pat said.

"No reason to be nervous, Padre! Actually, we've had Catholics in Dragomans for centuries. Under one of the earlier dictators, it was the Catholics, I'm pretty sure, who took over the Jewish quarter in the capital after the Jews were—"

"Oh, isn't that fascinating!" Fr. Pat said.

"Prin, can you see behind me?" Shahad asked.

"Yes, why?" Prin asked.

He could see great blue sky and square, washed-out limestone buildings and surprisingly close black mountains. But why was this Professor Shahad trying to distract him from whatever else was going on here? How did a Skype conversation about curriculum planning lead to, well, what, exactly?

"Can we get back to curriculum planning?" Prin asked.

"Of course, in a moment. But this is your Holy Week, yes? So, one of those mountains has a chapel that has something to do with the Passion of the Christ. Not Mel Gibson, the real thing, the, you know, what the Bible says happened. That mountain is said to be part of the story. Something happened there, at the time of the crucifixion," she said.

"Really? What's it called?" Prin said.

He wondered if the air was heavy and still in there. It must have been. Then what wind blew through? Did it still carry the saving breath of God or now only the smell of gasoline, gunsmoke, beard-sweat?

"Sorry, I don't know the details, I'm secular, what you call a 'none,' not a nun. Get it?" said Shahad.

Fr. Pat roared and slapped his knees so hard he bruised his palms on the titanium.

"Anyway, when you come here at the end of Ramadan to give your lecture on Kafka, we'll make sure you visit. Totally safe!" Shahad said.

Wende brushed past him to take control of the keyboard. She ended the call and smiled at Prin. Fr. Pat smiled at Prin, too. He was flanked by smiles.

"I'm not going over there," Prin said.

"Oh, come on, Prin, we all believe in you," Fr. Pat said.

"You have to, and I know you want to," Wende said.

Was she doing it on purpose? He remembered the last time she'd said that to him! But then suddenly all of it—the longing and the regret and the regret for the longing—all of it blew away. Prin looked around. He heard a rushing in his ears. He felt a sudden pulling at his chest, a reaching in, a telling he knew not how to tell.

He looked around.

Then he heard it. A voice. The Voice.

Go.

Go?

Go.

Was anyone else hearing this, feeling it? Were they noticing it, about him? But they were smiling the same way, Wende and Fr. Pat, and the screen where that great big black Biblical mountain had just flashed was now just a plain white blank. Something had happened there, long ago.

Something had happened here, too, just now.

16

"I HAVE TO go, and you know I don't want to," Prin said.

"*Do* I know that?" Molly asked.

The girls were well ahead of them as they walked home from church. It was Holy Thursday and a warm April night in Toronto. Most of the snow had melted into pocky grey-white ridges that lined the sidewalks. The leaves were but small black buds, shaking in the wind. Prin felt clammy all around. The weather was close, he'd been picked to have his feet washed by the priest and had done a poor job of drying off, the adult diaper he was wearing chafed, and also, oh yes, he was lying to his wife. He wanted to go to Dragomans. Or, he had been told.

The need to go had been with him since the end of the meeting, and throughout Holy Week. Hearing the voice— somehow in his head and not in his head, loud and clear but only to him, Hebrew but he knew what was said—put his heart off-beat, his mind off-kilter. What had happened was ... not what, but who. Who. Whom. The memory of it made him hold his breath, wait for someone to notice, someone to say something. He strained, but nothing else had happened since. There was only a ringing in his ears from straining to hear again. He didn't know how to tell Molly why he wanted to go to Dragomans. How to explain it, without sounding like a madman or a conniving jackass?

Had he really heard a voice? Really? A voice? No. Worse. Better. No, worse. He'd heard The Voice.

Yours.

But wait. That he had to go to Dragomans in July was also plainly true, mundanely true. After the Skype call, Fr. Pat and Wende together explained that the Minister had, unbidden, sent UFU an initial investment to demonstrate just how serious the government was in its desire to create a partnership. The investment reflected the government's recently taking back control of the country's oil refineries from a series of militias and Russians, and the initial money was enough, on its own, to pay the professors' salaries for the summer.

All that was asked for, in return, was a small show-of-good-faith: that a professor from Toronto come to Dragomans at the end of Ramadan to deliver a lecture and meet with prospective students. Prin was the obvious choice. Why is that? he'd asked. And then, before the ensuing compliments became outright lies, he interrupted Fr. Pat and said he thought faculty salaries were guaranteed for at least a year. Fr. Pat said they were guaranteed for the academic year, September to May. Prin complained that this distinction had never been made publicly and Fr. Pat said he couldn't believe that in spite of the school's dire situation, people still weren't reading his blog.

"Who else is going?" Molly asked.

"Wende," Prin said.

"I see," Molly said.

"But there's really nothing to worry about there, dear. She's not why I want to go. Besides, you already told me you're not concerned," Prin said.

"And I'm not," Molly said.

"Then what is it?" Prin asked.

"It's almost like you want me to be concerned. But we both know why I'm not. You're a faithful husband, Prin. I know that's true of your heart and your soul. Your trueness has never been in doubt for me," Molly said.

"I'm glad," Prin said.

"As for your body, well, because of the cancer—" Molly said.

"So that's what you and Wende talked about in the kitchen," he said.

"No! And it doesn't matter what we talked about. She doesn't matter. Even your not having a salary this summer doesn't matter. We could make ends meet. We could skip swimming lessons and Gregorian chant camp. We could go to Milwaukee and stay with my family. Whatever. What matters is that you're thinking of going to a Middle Eastern country that just had a civil war. What matters is that you've survived cancer and now you're willing to risk your life for, for what? For who?"

"Whom," he said.

She walked ahead, catching up with the girls. She didn't turn back. Sometimes Molly didn't enjoy being married to an English professor.

But he wasn't just being an English professor! He didn't know how to tell her who, whom. Whom. He had to go there for work, and he wanted to go, yes, for far more than work. And not because he could tell Wende wanted this, for whatever technically-useless-but-still-kind-of-flattering reason, or to help UFU, or even to help Mariam and her fellow Christian orphan Kafka readers, or even, *even* to visit a chapel that had something to do with the crucifixion. Yes and yes and yes and *yes*, but he still wanted to go for more than all of that.

Actually, no, that wasn't it at all.

Prin didn't want to go. It was risky, even dangerous all around. Prin, alone by his own little lights, didn't see any higher good in going. But that rushing in his ears, that pulling at his chest right after Wende had told him he had to go. That reaching in had left him with a sense of his life suddenly off-beat, off-kilter. And not thrown off by an enlarged and cancerous and then removed prostate or by the swishy spectre of an overseas trip with an ex-girlfriend, but thrown off because this something, this someone, wasn't his to keep balanced; because deep down it was firm, full, real, and far more than mere candle-flicker and mountain view.

He didn't want to go.

God wanted him to go.

His phone rang.

"Prin!" said Kingsley.

"Yes, Dad?" said Prin.

"Don't be late! The tournament begins at 12 pm tomorrow," said Kingsley.

"Sorry, Dad, what tournament?" asked Prin.

The phone was silent for a very long time. Or mostly silent: there was a great deal of bullish steam being blown through an angry old man's flared nostrils.

"Oh yes, right, the tournament! Wait, it's happening on Good Friday?" Prin said.

"NO! You need to be more ambitious in life, son! If we win the tournament it's going to be a Great Friday!"

17

"GOOD GAME," PRIN said.

"Good game," his Dad said.

They fist-bumped each other and their opponents and walked off the court.

"But next time, when I call the shot—"

"I let you call the shots, Dad," Prin said.

"Good son," Kingsley said.

For the last three hours, he'd been playing a game of over-sized ping pong with viciously competitive old men and their flabby sons. Kingsley and Prin were undefeated, so far.

He was starving, dizzy, and looking for a theologically respectable reason for how he was spending his Good Friday. Elsewhere, right now, Filipinos were volunteering to be nailed to crosses. Italians were dragging crosses across cobblestone. Americans were setting up thick, polished veneration crosses made of hypoallergenic wood. Molly and the girls were baking hot-cross buns for the homeless. Egyptians were deciding whether to venture out and Dragomanians were thinking this was a Pretty Good Friday—they weren't hiding in mountains or living in camps, at least. And Prin was wandering through a padded gymnasium, his eyes watering from all the antiphlogistine being applied around him.

How could he make this Friday Good again?

The only noise he could hear was a constant tapping—a half-dozen whiffle balls knocking against wooden paddles at long intervals—and also the gasps of men in sudden pain, stretching and lunging, hammering shots and being hammered right back. Prin closed his eyes. Forget a priest tapping on his watchface. *This* was the sound of the soldiers hammering nails into Christ's hands and feet as they hung Him on the cross. This day. This very day! Yes, and those gasps were the sound someone made from being hammered onto wood. And the sound of hammering someone onto wood.

Because how could you do that to any man and not gasp, too?

"Prin! What the hell! You're just standing there dreaming," Kingsley said.

"Sorry, Dad, it's just that it's Good Friday and—"

"Stop your Jimmy Swaggarting! Let's get going! I want to watch Kiwi Ken and his son on the far court. If they win we'll be playing against them in the final," Kingsley said.

Prin falls a second time.

Actually, he just slipped on his own sweat, lunging for a nasty little drop shot, but when he went down, he stayed down. Kingsley lashed his son's back with his racket. Then he stalked off the court. His mother came out of nowhere and kneeled beside him, pressing a perfumed cloth to his face. She was wearing a T-shirt that read

DON'T WORRY, BEYONCÉ

Lizzie shoved half a Snickers bar into his gasping mouth. He chewed and batted her concerned hands away from his gym shorts.

"Shhh, Eat. I know it's Good Friday, son, and I know you're fasting. Molly texted me that she was worried, so I came to bring you food. You didn't pull anything … down there … did you? Are you wearing a sport diaper? No one needs to know about this. Chew, chew, good boy. I told Kareem to stop filming when I came to you," said Lizzie.

"Hey! Kingsley! Mate, get junior's nursey mumsy off the court! Tell her she can breast-feed him during the trophy presentation. To us. It's still our serve. 11-4. Let's go!" said Kiwi Ken.

"Are you going to let these men speak that way about your own mother?" Kingsley asked.

Lizzie exited back to the bleachers as her ex-husband crowded over their fallen son.

"Would Jesus let someone speak that way about *His* mother? Also, these men are Anglicans! Anglicans are beating you, on Good Friday!" Kingsley said.

Grimacing, Prin got up from the lovely, cool floor and faced the giant, grinning, red-faced men standing across from them. This was the final game of the New Leaf Seniors' Centre First Annual Father-Son Pickleball tournament, which was sponsored by a downsizing firm and a local medical-supply store.

In games earlier that day, Prin had been amazed at how large and empty the other side of the pickleball court looked. But their prior opponents had been stumbling, swearing old men outfitted with elaborate back supports and shrugging, middle-aged sons. Neither could retrieve the deep-court lobs and simple drops and hard smashes to the side-courts that Kingsley and Prin delivered as they won game after game.

Whereas in the final, Kiwi Ken and Craig got to everything. They seemed to fill the whole world on the other side of the net with their slabby frames and endless arms and legs. They were both aging athletes—massive shoulders and thighs, industrial knee braces and sandbag waistlines that sagged heavy and hard.

Kiwi Ken pointed his racket menacingly at Kingsley.

"Still our serve. You ready ... Queensly?" he said.

He looked so small just then, small and defeated, his father. What could he say to that much white man, already up seven points against him? Prin loved his father. In spite of much, he loved him. Also, Prin suddenly had some sugar in him.

"Dad, I think the Aussie wants to know if you're ready for his serve," said Prin.

"Oy! What did you just call my dad?" said Kiwi Ken's son, Craig.

"You said Oy!" said Prin.

"I meant Ay! We say Ay! New Zealanders have been saying Ay for centuries! Anyway, Ay, you, five-foot-nothing four-eyes! I'll ask you again. What did you just call my dad? How'd you like it if I called your dad a bloody—Ow!"

Kiwi Ken smacked his son with his racket.

"Careful, son. You know what they're doing. Double standard in this country, never forget. You and I could be mistaken for used feminine papers, or even worse, for Australians, and no one would say boo. But if we said something off-colour, if you know what I mean, about our colourful friends across the net, we'd be disqualified from this tournament and probably kicked out of the country," said Kiwi Ken.

He glared over at Kingsley.

"Am I right ... Qu-Queensly? Shall we proceed? 11-4, four points to the championship. And aren't I telling the truth?" he asked.

"What is truth?" asked Kingsley.

His face was lit up like he'd just discovered a Holy Grail filled with lottery tickets.

"Yes, let's keep playing. So please put another shrimp on the barbee, Crocodile Ken Dundee," said Kingsley.

Kiwi Ken's serve went wide and out of bounds. After retrieving the ball with a new bounce in his step and then crouching to serve, Prin began singing "Tie me kangaroo down"—really only the first line, again and again. Kingsley sort of joined in and tapped with his orthopedic running shoes and then, from the front row of the impromptu and extremely sparse specta-tor's section, Lizzie and Kareem began to hum and mumble it too. While their own defeated sons checked their phones, the other seniors still watching joined in, a few of them clapping, thinking this was an approved activity.

Raging and red faced, Kiwi Ken and Craig began bobbling their heads and pretending to blow each other up while croon-ing "Thank you, come again!" in convenience-store accents after each point. Each lost point, that is.

Because their effort, well, sorry mates but oy, it boomeranged.

Because now Kingsley and Prin came at them again and again, darting and slamming and backhanding hard down the sidelines and clearing to the baseline before laying in feathery drops just over the net. The big men across from them lum-bered and whiffed, staggered and groaned and hit wide, hit long, hit net, raged and raged and raged at their opponents' Aussie antagonizing.

The score was tied, 12-12.

"I'm filing a complaint, Kingsley, to the management here, I'll have you know. This is bloody bush-league stuff and it may work in your Calcutta, but not in my Canada," said Kiwi Ken.

"Son, did you hear that? Waltzing Matilda is filing a com-plaint!" said Kingsley.

"Crikey!" said Prin.

"Let's hope for their sake they don't do a background check and find out Ken's grandparents were all convicts!" Kingsley said.

"I'M NOT A FUCKING AUSTRALIAN!"

"It's my serve, you jailbird son of a kangaroo."

18

HIS SERVING ARM in a sling and smiling as he hadn't in years, Kingsley held the victor's trophy with his free hand—Precious Moments father-and-son figurines hot-glued onto an old oaken hockey-trophy base. Kareem took pictures of him and of him with Prin, and even, once, of Kingsley and Lizzie and Prin. Kingsley thanked Lizzie for coming out to watch and also nodded, not un-warmly, at Kareem. Between pictures, Kareem said he was going to write to the Aga Khan Foundation and propose they build pickleball courts around the world.

Kingsley was very quiet in all of this. Here he was, for once, really winning at life. All these years getting from Sri Lanka to Canada, and all the struggle here, up through running the convenience store and losing his marriage and raising a son who wasn't an actual doctor. And the loneliness. But today he'd defeated white giants. He'd won a pickleball trophy. He had an obedient son, a proud ex-wife, and also a Muslim man asking for his advice on convincing the Aga Khan to make pickleball a priority of the faith. The comet could hit the Earth right now and he'd be fine. Because from existence, just then, what more could he expect, realistically? This was a damned good Friday.

"Let's celebrate!" said Kingsley.

"Dad, shouldn't we take you to a walk-in clinic just to make sure Kiwi Ken didn't break your arm when he tackled you?" asked Prin.

"It's just a strain. Maybe you can drive me to the restaurant and then, maybe someone else, I don't know who, but maybe someone else can drive your car," said Kingsley.

"Oh, me!" said Kareem.

"And then, then others can join us for dinner, if it's not against their religion," said Kingsley.

"Nothing is, except hate! Islam is a—"

"Okay, okay. Just come to dinner then," said Kingsley.

"Where should we go, Red Lobster?" asked Kareem.

"Ha! There's only one place to celebrate this victory, right Prin?" said Kingsley.

"Where's that, Dad?" asked Prin.

"Obvious! We're going to Outback Steakhouse!" said Kingsley.

Prin high-fived his father, who walked out of the gym humming a happy mash of "Waltzing Matilda" and "Tie Me Kangaroo Down."

Lizzie wiped her eyes and pulled Prin close.

"You know your father can't tell the difference between Catholic and catnip, so don't blame him. And I can still remember *status naturae lapsae simul ac redemptae* from convent school. But son, not even Pope Francis says we can have meat on Good Friday," Lizzie said.

But other than walking around each other at buffets after baptisms and first communions, his parents hadn't eaten together in years. Prin hadn't eaten with his parents, together, in years. Oh his heart ached in a way he didn't know was still possible, about his parents, for his parents, for the prospect of their being together just for an hour, never mind the new Muslim husband filming it all and his father's strategic ambiguity about the Sri Lankan matchmaker websites still showing up in his browser history.

Prin had to find a good reason to do this.

Christ didn't want to be nailed to the cross any more than Prin wanted to eat a well-done New York strip. But love, wasn't this done for love? Because he simply couldn't go to a steakhouse with his father and order the fish. It went against nature, against love.

But steak on Good Friday went against an even greater nature and love. He knew it didn't compare to hiding in caves and being blown up during your baby's baptism. But here, now, these too could be the great spiritual crises of a man's life! Because they were. Disappoint one father and make one mother cry, or do the same to another father and mother. He decided he would take up a cross made of charbroiled strip loins and accept a crispy crown of Bloomin Onion. Because yes we are fallen and at the same time we have been redeemed. Because it was 3 o'clock on Good Friday but it was already Easter Sunday, always.

19

"BLESS ME, FATHER, for I have sinned. But really, if you remember me, or at least my voice, I'm here for some advice, if you're still up for offering it," Prin said.

"Okay! But tell me your sins first, my son," the priest said.

He spoke in a sing-song way. This wasn't the same old man Prin had talked to the last time he'd come to this church. But you never know. And it was too late, anyway. He couldn't just skip out now that he was already kneeling.

"Father, the sin that weighs most heavily upon me is having just eaten meat," Prin said.

"On Good Friday! Naughty boy! Did you forget, somehow? It happens, I know. Back home in the Philippines, my grandmother used to always tell us *peccatum ad rem*, very bad! *Peccatum per accidens non est peccatum?* It's okay!" the priest said.

"No, Father, I ate it on purpose, fully knowing I was breaking the rule of abstinence," Prin said.

"Uh oh," said the priest.

"Yes. My own mother mentioned something she had learned in convent school, actually, about our natures being both fallen and at the same time—"

"Are you really going to blame your sins on your mother and her convent school memories? Here comes everybody living *la vida loca*, right? But anyways, you are saying you ate meat on Good Friday on purpose?" the priest asked.

"Yes," said Prin.

"That is a mortal si-in," the priest said.

"Yes, Father, and that is why I've come to confession. Shall I make an act of contrition now?" Prin asked.

"I thought you said you came here for some advice," the priest said.

"Well, yes, but actually it was related to another conversation that I had with a different priest here at the parish," Prin said.

"There is no other priest at this parish," he said.

"I was here a couple of weeks ago and spoke with a … Father Tom," Prin said.

"And so now you have broken the rule of abstinence, and you are lying to a priest. I have been the only priest here for three years," the priest said.

Prin ducked out of the burgundy drapery and looked around. This was absolutely the same church he'd come to after that first meeting with Wende and the others. If not a priest, who the hell had been sitting on the other side of this filigreed window screen?

"Father, I'm sorry, I'm not sure how to explain it. But you're sure there's no Father Tom associated with this parish?" Prin asked.

"Maybe many years ago, when all the priests here were Tom and Dick and Harry types. But not these days, sor-ry!" the priest said.

"So whatever absolution I received—probably isn't valid, right? He tapped his watch to remind me of my sins," Prin said.

"Oh, wait, that fellow! Yes! He's famous for doing that during confessions. I forgot, I took a group to Lourdes earlier this month and someone filled in for me. The Archdiocese must have sent Father Fernie. Father Tick-Tock Tom, we call him. Shhh, that's a secret," the priest said.

"Yes. Okay then. So, I wasn't lying to you, and I take it he's not here today, and I do have that one sin in particular to confess—eating meat on Good Friday. But what's really weighing on me, Father, is having to tell my wife something," Prin said.

"Uh oh. I don't like the sounds of that!" the priest said.

"Father, I have to go overseas for work, and it could be a dangerous trip, both in terms of the place I am going and the person I am travelling with, the woman I am travelling with, if you understand what I mean. The danger is at least in my heart and eye if not otherwise, due to a medical condition, but anyway, really, I don't want to go but —"

"Let me guess," the priest said.

There came a long, long pause.

"God wants you to go," the priest said.

Where had the sing-song gone?

"Father, it seems like you've heard this before, but—"

"And also what you just said, and what you're going to say next, what you all say next," the priest said.

What was Prin going to say next? He didn't know. How could this priest know? How could he know Prin had heard a voice? The Voice? Yours?

"So, say it. Say that the stripper really likes you and you're concerned about her and her kids and that she's actually an exotic dancer who wanted to be a ballerina when she was a little girl. You know this because you talk. You text. Say that you're just doing research and that's why you're looking at those pictures. Say you're taking the money because you're planning to give it to charity," the priest said.

"It's not like that at all!" Prin said.

"Bingo again! Next, you'll say that really you don't want to do something, something that will probably get you in trouble, get your family in trouble, get your soul in trouble, but you think God wants you to do it, and you're such a good Catholic boy and so you don't want to disobey God. And now you want me to tell you it's okay to do what you really want to do. But does God really want you to do this? And before you answer, remember the Third Commandment," the priest said.

"I am not going to commit adultery!" Prin said.

"That's the Seventh," the priest said.

"I meant taking the Lord's name in vain!"

Jesus, how could he get that wrong? Why did he get that wrong?

"So, now that we're talking the same commandment, go on," the priest said.

"Look Father, something really happened. I'm convinced I felt God's presence a little while ago, and that it moved me to do this, that He has moved me to do this. I heard Him. He … spoke to me," Prin said.

"Then why not just tell your wife?" the priest asked.

That was it? No jumping out of the confessional to dial 911 or the Vatican?

"Because she probably won't believe me, and for the same reason you don't believe me," Prin said.

"What I believe about you doesn't matter. Even what she believes doesn't matter. EVEN what you believe doesn't matter," the priest said.

"Then?" Prin asked.

"If we could ask Him, right now, on today of all days, what He believes about you?" the priest asked.

"Are you still there?" the priest asked.

"I am," Prin said.

"So tell me, what does God believe about you, right now, and always, no matter what you believe about Him or believe He's told you to do?" the priest asked.

"Father, I don't know. I'm sorry. I don't know. How can I know, how can any of us know? Look, I just came in here because I ate steak on Good Friday and also because I need to tell my wife something strange but true. I still do," Prin said.

"Whatever it is, it can't be stranger or truer than what God believes about you," the priest said.

20

MILWAUKEE. IT WAS the third of July, and as one of many, many compromises involved with Prin's travel plans, the family had come to stay with Molly's mother for the summer. He had told her the real reason he wanted to go to Dragomans, the Real reason, and she took it in without much trouble at all. They'd been discussing it ever since, including the fact that Prin could not point to any sense of Divine wish or desire since that first and only moment he'd heard. Was this God's silence, and was it to be taken as final? Or—and this was Molly's position—had Prin heard what he wanted to hear, and now he wasn't interested in hearing anything else? Molly thought surviving prostate cancer had turned Prin into a holy romantic.

"Why do you need to go to extremes to prove yourself worthy of God's love and attention, Prin?" she asked.

"But isn't that what we're supposed to do? Maybe it makes me a holy fool, but I think there's a great tradition of that," Prin said.

"I'm not sure it's even possible, dear, to prove ourselves so worthy. And yes, we should all try, but why can't you try closer to home? Why can't someone else be sent?" Molly asked.

"Because no one else heard what I heard," he said.

"How do you know?" she asked.

"So you want me to begin canvassing colleagues?" he asked.

"No, but—"

"Look, we've gone over this many times, Molly. It's just a week, and the State Department has lifted its travel warning about Dragomans, and do you really think the government over there, or the people at UFU, or Wende, want to risk this totally failing by putting a professor in harm's way?" said Prin.

"Maybe you are a holy fool," she said.

"I'm glad you're beginning—"

"Or maybe you're just a fool," she said.

In silence they finished making four stacks of towels and swimwear and associated goggles and caps and sprays and toys for a trip to a city pool with the cousins.

An hour later, Prin lifted a squirming, yuddering daughter into each of his arms and backed away from the giant black man screaming at him, at his children, at everyone, to Get out! Wearing a stretched-out tank top he rampaged around the edge of the kidney-shaped pool. It took Prin a moment to realize that the body the other lifeguards were dealing with, on the far side of the deep end, belonged to one of his nephews, fourteen-year-old John-Paul.

How could this have happened? What could have happened? Five minutes before, two days into their stay with Molly's family, they'd been in the midst of a perfect American summertime. Slow and muggy, a big blue sky, plans to go out for custard after everyone went swimming. Then they'd go back to Molly's sister's elephantine brick-and-vinyl house for grilled brats and a family rosary in the great room and then FaceTime with the dad on a business trip and Skype with the dad in Iraq, and then more custard and YouTube videos, all in polar-frigid central air.

None of that seemed possible now, even though, just five minutes before, John-Paul and his little brother Ignatius and their cousin Juan Diego had been bobbing around him and his girls, sleek as seals and snickering about some plan they were hatching. They gave each other shoulder punches and high-fives and raced into the deep end. And now one of them was lying on the hard tiles, with lifeguards attending him while his cousins stood off to the side, hands over their mouths.

The chief lifeguard was down on her knees beside the boy's body, tapping his cheek and checking vitals. She threw back her ponytail, preparing to administer CPR. Prin prayed for his nephew. He also noted the tawny magnificence of the lifeguard's nape and shoulders as she bent down to breathe life back into his nephew.

He felt nothing. He continued to feel nothing.

Which was great.

He was grateful to have been made forever safe like this, for a week away with Wende. For months now, they'd continue exchanging messages on VaultTok. All the rereading in the world confirmed these were only businesslike. There had been one reference to keeping him abreast of developments, but he was probably just reading into it. And in hopes of what? A temptation he would then have to overcome?

He didn't even find Wende that attractive anymore. And meanwhile there was all of this non-worrying about non-worry, instead of praying intently for the boy—wasn't he the godfather to this one? How awful that he didn't remember just then—while whipping his pleading kids this way and that way so they wouldn't see whatever was happening. But he could.

"JOHN-PAUL!" his mother said.

But Prin's heart didn't buckle and join her pain. It lifted. It eased and sang. Her tone was angry, very angry. She had her oldest son by the ear. He was standing, he was alive, he was wincing and laughing and the lifeguards were walking behind him, to the pool office. The chief lifeguard was at the very back of the scrum. She was six-feet tall, chestnut ponytail, high cheekbones, bee-stung lips, doe eyes, red short shorts, all of her twenty-one years dipped in days of summer sun. She had her arms crossed over the uppermost contents of her gravity-defying swimsuit. And she didn't look angry, or amused, but something else.

Of course!

If Prin were a teenage boy bobbing around a pool staffed by an Amazonian Venus and not a snipped-out forty-year-old playing mermaid castle in the shallows, maybe he'd fake a drowning too.

And of course this was worth a mother's vengeance, and a grandmother's wondering out loud while dishing out custard what his sainted papal namesake must be thinking in heaven. It was also worth the mumbling, awkward confession he'd have to make to their friendly, super-cool young family priest, who would grant God's forgiveness for all the trouble he'd caused, for all the secret pleasure he'd taken in making trouble: because what else is sin? Of course it was worth it, Prin thought. Not just the lips, but the story of how the boy touched those lips, a story to tell for the rest of the summer.

Prin stopped studying gravity's rainbows. Off to the side, he saw Molly lecturing the other boys, who were doing their best to feel bad that Aunty Molly was so totally disappointed in them. They were mostly failing. They had a pretty good summer story to tell, too.

"Daddy, is John-Paul in trouble? Is Aunty Elizabeth taking him to the hospital?" asked Maisie.

"Daddy, can you put us down now? Can we go back into the pool and play Elsa mermaid pony underwater castle again and this time can you be Olaf?" asked Maisie.

"No, I want Daddy to play Elsa marries piss-side down!" said Pippa.

"It's Poseidon, Poseidon, love," said Prin.

21

LATER THAT EVENING, while he waited for his turn to Skype, Prin decided he couldn't talk to his nephews about what had happened at the pool that day. But only he had seen the lifeguard's face as she walked the others to the office, where his nephew John-Paul's membership card was cut in half for his fake-out and where he was given a summer-long ban from the pool. Only Prin saw that she wasn't exactly angry, and she wasn't exactly amused. You could camp out on the question of what that lifeguard had been thinking for the rest of the summer! If only he could tell them, at least give them this gift as they headed out that night to the dank summer fort they'd built in the little woods behind the house.

Prin wanted to tell his nephews about the lifeguard so very badly, and probably for the same reason he wished Wende had ulterior motives in letting him know that her seat assignment for their upcoming flight to Dragomans was 34C. Not that he wanted to act on these wants. He certainly hadn't been acting on anything at bedtime with Molly since his surgery, and she really didn't seem to mind. Hugs and pecks, pecks and hugs. Not even her leg lying upon his midriff anymore, that long, dark night of the groin.

What Prin wanted, really, was to suffer, to struggle with not acting, not looking, not telling, not thinking, not imagining what he knew he shouldn't. He wished he'd been at least a little moved by seeing that lifeguard! He was old enough now that attraction to a woman was more complicated than that, but it started and ended in the same place. And he wasn't there anymore. No one moved him. Only God had moved him, and that was to go to Dragomans. That was it, and that had to be enough.

"Uncle Prin, it's your turn!" said another of his nephews.

"Thanks, Xavier," Prin said.

He high-fived the boy, who quickly recomposed his face as he exited the study, and his Skype time with his faraway, pixelated father, to rush outside. There, he took it all out on whoever was blocking his path to the backyard zip line.

"Hi Patrick!" Prin said.

His brother-in-law was sitting at a computer terminal in a warehouse-sized army facility in Baghdad. People in fatigues were walking around behind him. In the far background were blobby, bright squares of pure light—either portly angels or Iraqi daylight.

"So, what time is it over there?" Prin asked.

"Five minutes later than the last time I was asked that question," said Patrick.

"Right. Sorry," Prin said.

"Don't worry about it," said Patrick.

Having recomposed his face after seeing one of his boys, he flashed fresh, stay-positive smiles.

"Prin! Good to see you! So man, what's going on? I hear the surgery worked out, yeah?"

"Yes. Thanks. How are things with you?" Prin asked.

"Can't complain … meaning, I can't complain on hardware belonging to the US military that's probably being monitored by Russian hackers!" Patrick said.

"But is the whole project coming along?" Prin asked.

Patrick nodded and ran a hand along his heavy jaw.

"It's not easy, I can say that. But wow, thanks for asking. I gotta say, I was pretty surprised you even wanted to chat," Patrick said.

"I'm just really interested in hearing more about your experiences over there," Prin said.

He didn't sound that hollow, did he? He'd known his brother-in-law for years. They were on fine terms, but little more. Was it Prin's fault he wasn't much for competitive woodworking? Was it Patrick's fault he wasn't much for animality studies?

"Right. Well, what I can say, truly, is that we're working with some good people here on the ground, people who want to make this happen. And I can't believe I'm actually saying this, but some of our Scandinavian colleagues are proving really helpful. I don't think we really agree on what a new legal code for Iraq should and shouldn't involve, but they're kind of a good go-between for my team and our Iraqi colleagues," Patrick said.

"I know you can't say a lot, but do you have any advice for someone going into these kinds of situations?" Prin asked.

His heart began beating faster.

"What do mean?" Patrick asked.

"In a couple of weeks I'm going to Dragomans," Prin said.

"Come again?" said Patrick.

"Yeah, I'm going to the Middle East too. I'm going to Dragomans for work, on behalf of the university. We're working with some people over there to create a university for young people coming out of the civil war," Prin said.

"Coming out of the civil war, you mean, like it's finished? Prin, you sure you know what you're doing? Do you know the situation you're getting into over there?" said Patrick.

"Well, the university has hired a consultant, and I'm going over with her," Prin said.

"I repeat my question," said Patrick.

"Look, Patrick, I'm there for three days, to meet some people— all US citizens, professors with family ties to the place, who've gone back to help out, and also some of their local students," said Prin.

"I repeat my question," said Patrick.

"Well, um, I want to help some persecuted Christians get educations?" Prin said.

"Sorry. All good people, I'm sure. Listen, they are good people. It's not them. It's the other people who've gone back there to help out. You know what I mean, right?" said Patrick.

"I do, and sorry, please, please correct me if I'm wrong, but Dragomans is a peaceful and stable country, correct?" said Prin.

Patrick took a sip of bottled water and nodded.

"In the context of former military dictatorships in the Middle East and North Africa, yes, your account of Dragomans, at present, meaning right now, while we're Skyping, is accurate. Just remember that over here, peaceful and stable can turn to hellfire and bodies hanging from bridges just like that. My wife loves her baby sister. My sweet little Toronto nieces need a dad. So Prin, I'm just saying, don't be stupid," said Patrick.

"I won't," said Prin.

"Easy for you to say. I'll be praying for you, buddy. Just like I hope you do for me," said Patrick.

"We offer up a Hail Mary for Uncle Patrick every night before bed," said Prin.

"Great. I have long days of meetings and then late nights of filing reports for Washington. In all that, I feel those prayers, I really do," said Patrick.

"That's great," Prin said.

Where was the admiration for what he was doing? Not that he was doing it for that reason. But still. If great big Patrick believed Prin was doing something heroic, even if he waited a week before telling Molly, he could beam. His soul could skip through God's backyard sprinkler.

"Prin? Are you still with me? Don't make me yell what I just said," said Patrick.

"Sorry, just repeat it," said Prin.

"I was talking about the situation at the pool today. And, between you, me and the minarets, good for John-Paul, right?

I'm assuming the lifeguard in question was worth the collateral damage he sustained," said Patrick.

"And then some," Prin said.

He waited, but nothing.

"And this stays on the down-low," said Patrick.

"Deal!" said Prin.

He said it with vigour, but it was all and only in his voice.

"Okay. Good talk. The things you miss out on, you can't ever imagine until you hear about them," said Patrick.

"Yes, I'm sure you must—"

"Listen. When you're in Dragomans, watch out for people jogging with serious faces, people not making any noise. I can't really explain what I mean by that, but you'll know when you see it. And I pray you don't see it. You know these are not jogging cultures, right? And it's always so damned hot, and no one's ever in a hurry to get anywhere. So the runners stick out. And Prin, get away if you see any of them. That's it, man. That's the sum total of my personal-security advice based on four months in Iraq," said Patrick.

"Thanks, Patrick. I appreciate it," said Prin.

"Good. And yeah, okay, good for you, too, doing something like this! It's risky, but worth it. Alright Uncle Prin, send in the next contestant!" said Patrick.

On his soul-skipping way out of the study, Prin bent down and high-fived his niece Mary-Angelica, who ran in and jumped on the swivel chair, which immediately bucked and swung around. She told Prin to stay back as she steadied herself, and when she did, she seemed extremely proud of herself. Only then did she really study the screen and remember there was more to this visit to her father's study than riding his chair. Prin left once she clapped and squealed and began smudging her daddy's glassy, smiling face with static-sparkly kisses.

Close to midnight, Molly lying beside him, Prin was still awake. He pulled one of her legs on top of him, and right away she pulled the rest of herself warm and close.

He waited.

She kissed him on the cheek and said she liked that he wanted her close to him. He waited. She reminded him that they had to be careful, and not just because of his surgery. Her mother was sleeping in the next room. Molly slipped off and snuggled beside him. Prin wanted to remind her of all those times they'd lain here and not been careful, had risked it, because they'd wanted each other—that closeness, that crush, that fullness and oneness and life beyond, yes, beyond even God randomly rushing through his ears and trilling his heart in the middle of a meeting. The doctors had told him about this consequence, and he and Molly had long since agreed pills were insulting, yet Prin had no idea how much he'd come to miss being a man alive.

Propped up in bed, he began reading blogs, many of them Google-translated into English from Arabic, French, and German: "The old homes of today will be the gravity of tomorrow. We are the liberty for tomorrow. Just wait mercy. God has the most mercy names." What mattered was that Dragomans was peaceful, it was stable, and there was nothing he could find, even on page twenty of his search, to suggest otherwise.

This was, technically, reassuring.

How could his brother-in-law Patrick offer anything but pure precaution? He was a Milwaukee-born constitutional lawyer working in Iraq: how could he not point out every possible risk? Which weren't many.

Which was, again, technically, reassuring.

Prin had a greater chance of being gored to death by a rhinoceros in Toronto than he did of being killed by a terrorist in Dragomans, according to a disaster-scenario generator he found before finally falling asleep to vague dreams of a snowy zoo, a rhino on the loose.

22

THE NEXT MORNING, the Fourth of July, everyone went to the mall. Everything was star spangled and 50 percent off the lowest-ticketed price. Molly and her two sisters and all the girl cousins set out with canvas bags full of canvas bags. Prin, who, with the others out of town, was the ranking uncle, had clearance to take the boys to a matinee. *Transformers: Terror Alliance* had just opened, and the stars of the WNBA spent much of the movie lunging around in shredded titanium spandex. Nevertheless, Prin was still surprised at the size of the crowd gathered in front of the escalator to the movieplex.

"Hello Milwaukee! Hello America!"

A big man was calling out to the crowd. He had a face like a beefsteak tomato. He was wearing a T-shirt with crescent blades and crescent moons floating around the word HISTORY, which was written across it in Arabic-style letters with a giant STOP sign stamped overtop. He was standing on a small stage set up between two cellphone sales kiosks staffed by swarthy, spiky-haired young men in ill-fitting dress shirts and loose belts and shiny ties. They were watching while eating their lunch from styrofoam containers.

"Hello Schlaffler!" the crowd called back.

"Oh, Uncle Prin, can we watch this?" his nephew Juan-Diego asked.

"What is it?" asked Prin.

"What is it? Seriously? It's Schlaffler, Uncle Prin! His radio show's on every night, between Hannity and Rush. They don't play it in Toronto?" asked his nephew, Xavier.

"No," said Prin.

"Mom hates him," said his nephew John-Paul.

"Yeah, but moms only listen to NPR," said Juan-Diego.

"National Pointless Radio!" said all of his nephews.

"I'm guessing he's a right-wing radio guy?" Prin asked.

"He's a reality-check radio guy, Uncle Prin," Xavier said.

"But Mom complains when he's on, so we listen while Dad's driving us to practice or we podcast it in the garage," John-Paul said.

"Hey folks! Question for ya. Who gets the last laughter?" asked Juan-Diego.

"Schlaffler!" said his other nephews.

A moment later, the man on stage asked the same question and the crowd called out the same answer.

"Guys, we're going to miss the trailers if we don't go up to the theater now," said Prin.

He didn't like the crowd, which was, for the most part, beefy men in beards and Green Bay Packer caps taking pictures of Schlaffler with phones fitted out in thick rubber cases. The few women in attendance had, in general, no facial hair, and their cases were pink rather than jet black or black and dump-truck yellow; otherwise, they looked and weighed about the same. Prin could say he wanted to leave because he knew his sisters-in-law wouldn't approve, but he knew his nephews would counter that their dads would have let them stay for the rally before launching into a *Come on, Uncle Prin*. Their adolescent American voices, golden, pure, and cracking like the Liberty Bell, would have tolled hard in his ears, his professorial, sonless, brotherless, ethnic Toronto ears. *Come on, Prin, be a normal guy for once.*

"Okay, we can stay for a few minutes and then go to the movie," said Prin.

They all high-fived him and Prin felt great and at one with America, this ham and savage land where people actually said things like

"USA! USA! USA!"

"My fellow patriots, who's ready to meet a great American hero?" asked Schlaffler.

"USA! USA! USA!"

"Welcome to our Honor American Heroes Rally at Plymouth Heights Mall. A quick thank you to our sponsors, Greinke Auto Detailing and Accenture. And now, it gives me great pleasure to introduce you to Bryan 'Big Bear' Kowalski, who did tours in Iraq and Afghanistan with the greatest army on earth before returning home to Wisconsin to find out his job at the local paper mill got folded up and mailed to Mexico," said Schlaffler.

"BOO!"

"But did he just give up and get on the Democrats' welfare-wagon-to-nowhere?" asked Schlaffler.

"NO!"

"That's right. He tried to re-enlist. But guess what? Those chicken hawks and turkey vultures and plain old turkeys in Washington had just passed more cutbacks to our armed forces, so there was no re-enlisting. Okay, I know what you're thinking: *now* he gets on that Washington welfare wagon. Right? WRONG!" said Schlaffler.

"USA! USA! USA!"

"Guess what this guy did? With beautiful wife Jenny and new baby girl Dakota and three-year-old son Barron at home, he went back over using his own family's savings! He joined some freedom fighters in Syria, took on the radical Muslim jihadi crusaders in basically the most dangerous part of the world, and now he's come home, and he's decided to join us here, today, at Plymouth Heights Mall, to tell us all about it. He's going to be on the Schlaffler Show tonight as well, 7 pm on WXUSA 1850 and Sirius 145, so tell all your friends and enemies to tune in. Yes, right before the birthday of our great nation, a beacon of freedom in a world of darkness, we're going to hear from a red-blooded beacon of Bravery and Freedom. Ladies and gentlemen, let's have a Schlaffler DefCon 1 welcome for my friend, my personal hero, Brian 'Big Bear' Kowalski!" said Schlaffler.

·A big guy with an embarrassed smile climbed onto the stage, gave a thumbs-up to the crowd, and awkwardly bear-hugged Schlaffler, who then stood back, took off his Schlaffler Show cap and placed it on his heart. He saluted the young man. Everyone in the crowd did the same.

"So, 'Big Bear,' what can you tell us about the situation over there?" asked Schlaffler.

"First of all, Schlaffler, I just want to thank you and all of you here today for your support. When I was over there, you know, fighting, giving 110 percent, knowing that I had people like all of you believing in me and what I was doing, it just helped a lot with the adversity," said Kowalski.

"So yeah, okay, tell us about that adversity, Brian," said Schlaffler.

"Well, yeah, you know, it's pretty complicated, all the different groups fighting each other. And sometimes they fight, you know, one group's members start fighting each other, and then the Russians and Turks and Iranians and us get all mixed up in it too. Pretty confusing," said Kowalski.

"But basically, they all hate America, right?" asked Schlaffler.

"No. No way!" said Kowalski.

"Seriously?" said Schlaffler.

"The rebel group I was with, man, they just love America," said Kowalski.

"USA! USA! USA!"

"That's not what the so-called mainstream media tells us, with its so-called facts and truths, you know, Brian," said Schlaffler.

"Right. But, well, I went over and helped train a group of Christian militia fighters who were trying to protect their village because the national army and the coalition people basically weren't doing anything and they had the terrorist militias making incursions all the time," said Kowalski.

"Wow. That's, you know, personally, to know, you know, the Bible says, 'Where two or three are gathered in my name.' Even there, in the Middle East, it's true, huh? So Brian, did you all pray together?" asked Schlaffler.

"Actually, when we weren't training, mostly we just talked about football," said Kowalski.

"Are you kidding me?" asked Schlaffler.

"No!" said Kowalski.

"Okay, but when you say football, you mean soccer, like the Europeans call it, right?" asked Schlaffler.

Here Schlaffler held his hands out in mincing fashion and did an off-balance dainty dance to hoots from the growing crowd.

"No, when I say football, I mean, you know, football. When I first got there, this one guy, Muktar, I called him Mookie, anyway, he asked me where I was from, and I said Neenah, Wisconsin, up near Green Bay. And Mookie smiles and does the Aaron Rogers touchdown move, you all know it, the Championship Belt," said Kowalski.

Schlaffler, Big Bear, and everyone in the crowd pantomimed buckling up a giant belt to their heavy hips. Prin kept his hands vaguely on his waist.

"NO KIDDING!" said Schlaffler.

"That's right. Anyway, before we went out on perimeter duty together that first night, Mookie says to me, 'The Packers are America's team!'" said Kowalski.

At that, the mall crowd went wild and stayed wild for a long while. They died down just as Prin saw two bearded men in ballcaps and long coats running towards the stage from the side. They had serious faces. They were wearing long coats in July. Weren't those serious faces? What did Patrick say about men running with serious faces? In a mall in Milwaukee, on the Fourth of July, were those serious, bearded faces and long coats?

"THEY'VE GOT GUNS!"

Prin was knocked down and someone trampled his arm. From near the stage he heard a snapping sound, shots fired. He got up and could only see two of his nephews knocking about as people scrambled in all directions. Someone grabbed his arm, hard—thank God, the third nephew. He reached into a mass of moving, screaming bodies. He pulled one of his other nephews towards him; the other pushed and found him, but he didn't know which way to go with them, it was like they were stuck in a wind turbine. Whoever had the guns, my God, where were they now?

Molly and the girls.

But with the crush of plump, pulsing bodies, his nephews gripping his arms—he couldn't run for them if he tried. And still he tried, dragging his nephews with him, pushing and pushing to get to empty space and hide them and run as fast as he could, in an unknown direction, to save his wife and children from unknown gunmen. His face squished into the hot Easter ham of someone's tank-top bared shoulder and he turned his face and that's when his eyes went back to the stage and he saw Schlaffler down on one knee, his hat knocked off and his bald head blood-spattered.

Under the mall lights, his blood ran hot pink.

23

"BACK TO OUR continuing coverage of today's Terror at Plymouth Heights Mall. What we know so far is that, shortly before 2 pm, two anti-war activists staged a terrorism-style attack on popular conservative talk-radio personality Perry Schlaffler. They shot him with a series of fluorescent paint-ball bullets, and in the process disrupted his rally to celebrate a Wisconsin veteran who recently returned from fighting radical Islamists in Syria. In an odd twist, the assailants were tackled by the veteran himself and are now under heavy police guard at Columbia-St. Mary's Hospital as they recover from their injuries. The veteran, twenty-nine-year-old Brian Kowalski, a Neenah native and recently divorced father of two, was questioned by authorities then released. He was unavailable for comment. Two employees of a cellphone supplies kiosk near the attack site were also questioned and released by authorities. A dozen people sustained minor injuries.

"In a YouTube video released shortly after the attack began, the activists claimed their actions were meant to draw attention to Post-Traumatic Stress Disorder among returning soldiers and to the need for increased funds for wellness counselling and advanced research in this area. Unconfirmed reports suggest the accused are former graduate students from the University of Wisconsin-Madison. University officials have no comment.

Plymouth Heights Mall will be closed for the rest of the week, mall officials are saying, while law enforcement conducts its investigation. Damage and lost revenue are predicted to run into the millions. And if you're wondering about Schlaffler himself, well, he was on the air as usual tonight. He promises his next Rally for American Heroes will be even bigger and reminds his listeners that he always gets the last laughter. He also says he'll keep his head painted pink until October to raise money for breast cancer. Now let's look at some more viewer-supplied cellphone footage of that chaos before returning to national network coverage."

"Look, Prin! That's you and the boys! Oh now look at my grandsons. They look like lost little lambs," said Molly's mother.

To Molly's mother, a retired Montessori teacher, all children basically looked like lost little lambs. But in the blur and shake of a cellphone video, you could see how terrified the boys were, hanging on to each other and to Prin. Molly and the girls had been at the far, far end of the mall, along with Molly's sisters and their daughters, all of them going through no-return steep-discounted bedding and pillows in the basement of Macy's. They heard nothing, knew nothing, until Molly's mother called to see if they were okay. Around then the mall's fire alarms went off and it went from there.

Prin would have called right after all the running around had stopped, but his nephews wouldn't let go of his hands for even a moment—and he didn't get upset with them, American teenage boys crying in public. In fact, Prin vowed he would never tell a soul, which was pointless now that their red puffy faces were beaming into television screens across the city. Would they be able to boast about being there when it happened? What if someone shared a devastating screenshot? At least they still had the chief lifeguard's lips.

24

"PRIN, I DON'T think you should go to Dragomans," said Molly.

"Really Molly? Because my parents both called to say they think we shouldn't come to Milwaukee anymore," said Prin.

"That's ridiculous," said Molly.

"I agree. So what's changed that now you think I shouldn't go to Dragomans?" asked Prin.

"What happened today," said Molly.

"What happened today, Molly, in Milwaukee, at the mall you've been going to your whole life? Because of a right-wing talk-radio idiot and some paint-balling left-wing goons? That makes no sense," said Prin.

Standing in the kitchen, they were both quiet, making all the more noticeable the gruesome sound of Molly cutting through the veins of a grapefruit and dropping the pieces into bowls.

"Okay, sorry dear," Prin said.

"Sorry about what, exactly? About constantly trying to make me not worry about your going to the Middle East with your ex-girlfriend?" asked Molly.

"So you are worried!" said Prin.

"Yes! But not about her, not about you and her. I'm worried about you, about why you want to go over there," said Molly.

"Dear, I've told you, it's not me—"

"It's God. Right," said Molly.

"So you don't believe me!" said Prin.

"This is what I know: I don't want you to go. Your wife, the mother of your children, she doesn't want you to go. Isn't that enough? How could that not be enough for you? For God?" asked Molly.

"You think something like this could happen there?" asked Prin.

"Why go across the world to court disaster?" asked Molly.

"Because these days it can find you just as easily around the corner from your mother's house, dear. We're all courting disaster by getting out of bed in the morning, by going to the mall, by going to the zoo. Remember?" said Prin.

She gutted another grapefruit.

"Molly, nothing's going to happen. The government over there has too much invested in this to risk it going wrong. And I'm reading everything I can find online about Dragomans. I even asked Patrick when we Skyped yesterday—"

"And what did he think?" asked Molly.

"Well, it's Patrick," said Prin.

"Meaning, he said you shouldn't go, right?" said Molly.

"Not exactly. He just gave me some advice for how to avoid risks while I'm over there. For seventy-two hours, I'll remind you again, and almost all of those seventy-two hours will be spent behind the security gates at the airport, or behind the security gates at the government building where we're holding the class, or behind the security gates at a government hotel," said Prin.

"All of those are targets," said Molly.

"True, they are—anywhere in the world, Molly. I really think you're just shaken up by what happened today, which, in the end, was really nothing, correct?" said Prin.

"What if it's a warning? I mean, like you said—first the lemurs, now this," said Molly.

"A warning from who?" asked Prin.

"Whom," said Molly.

"Are you saying God decided to use a dead lemur, and then Perry Schlaffler and two grad-school dropouts, to warn me not to give a lecture on Kafka in the Middle East? Listen, believe me, and I really mean believe me, Molly, when I say I think God has ways more blunt and more subtle of letting us know His will," said Prin.

She spat out a grapefruit seed.

25

A WEEK LATER, they took him to the airport. Prin told the girls he was just off to give another boring professor lecture in some boring place, and then he'd come home, yes, with Tic Tacs for everyone. Molly smiled and stayed quiet. For days now, the two of them had been very quiet. She had wanted him to stay back, and that wasn't enough.

"I'll be home soon, girls!" said Prin.

He turned towards the departure gate.

"Daddy, you promise?" Maisie called out.

"Prin! Answer her!" Molly said.

She said this playfully, for the sake of the children. Almost playfully.

"PRIN!"

Part Two

26

"ARE WE THERE yet?" Prin asked.

"Yes, for sure," the driver said.

"But you keep saying that," Prin said.

"That's because it keeps being true!" the driver said.

"Okay," Prin said.

"Okay?" the driver said.

"Okay," Prin said.

"OKAY!" the driver said.

"Okay," Prin said.

"Good," the driver said. Then he turned on the radio. Taylor Swift. He turned up the volume.

They were stuck in traffic somewhere in the capital city. All around them were delivery trucks and buses and scooters and taxis. Everyone was honking and moving very slowly under a hard white sun and brilliant blue sky. Traffic cops in maroon berets stood in the middle of narrow intersections, their brown uniforms sweated through. Close by, on either side of the narrow road, were old square limestone buildings now faded and cracked and patched here and there, their ground floors chockablock with market stalls made from corrugated metal painted red and blue and green. The narrow walkways beside the jammed road were crowded with old, gap-toothed men sitting and standing around little tables full of teacups and pulled-apart newspapers. Small silver radios shot sunlight from certain angles.

There were a few women as well. They were covered and round and weighed down with shopping bags spilling the floppy tops of vegetables and, in more than one case, pair of bound-up chicken feet. Each followed behind a bored-looking man talking on a phone. Some were bored-looking boys. Two kinds of young men were standing around everywhere and ignoring each other: the first were leather-jacketed and jeans-wearing, all strutty and square-shouldered and smoking and snorting at each other like background players in a *Grease* revival; the other were thin young men concerned with looking extremely pious, a few of them wore long beige robes, all of them sported cuffed pants and brown parsley beards. The more-important-looking ones kept rubbing their foreheads, which had little dent marks, and picked their teeth with thick, ginger-coloured twigs.

From the apartments above the stalls and walkways children peeked out here and there, sometimes calling to each other but mostly just staring down and around. One boy appeared to be staring at Prin, who thought and thought and thought and then waved. The kid waved back right away. Then he disappeared and came back with a soccer ball, which he proudly showed to Prin. But before Prin could give him a thumbs-up, someone called the kid away and the window went black. Prin still wasn't sure if he was going to live or die in Dragomans.

The driver honked again, again in vain, and then adjusted his rear-view mirror to mug an apologetic face at Prin. He knocked the golden charm dangling from the mirror. It was shaped like a three-fingered hand and had a yellow-jewelled eyeball in the middle.

"Sorry, sir. Traffic is always like this close to the government buildings. Lots of security checks. Shouldn't be much longer," the driver said.

"Good to know. Can you turn down the music? And is this the only route?" Prin said.

"Sorry, I love the Taylor Swift. This is the only good route. All the diplomats and VIPs like you use this route, sir. Bill

Clinton uses it when he comes to give the speeches. You don't believe me?" the driver asked.

"About Bill Clinton? Yes, I believe you," Prin said.

"I believe you too," the driver said.

He turned and smiled and nodded and turned the music back up. Prin felt vertiginous, jet-lagged, and more nervous than he probably needed to be while taking in his shaky, refracted self in the mirror-squares of the driver's sunglasses, the eye of the charm shaking below. And why exactly did this driver, or Shane from the zoo, or Fr. Pat, believe in him? What did he believe about himself, just now? Was he truly a VIP? What made him a VIP? To who? Whom? Oh yes, that's right. He still didn't know what God believed about him, but even if nothing and no one else was warming and filling and moving his very being to remind him of it, Prin could remind himself of it.

He should be not afraid.

He hadn't come here just to lecture orphans and keep his job. He sat up a little straighter in the backseat of the frigid, loud, leathery airport sedan.

"So, how would you rate the current security conditions situation in Dragomans?" he asked.

"Wow, you sound like you work for CNN!" the driver said.

"Thanks. I'm actually just a professor," Prin said.

"Not just! Not just! And please, I'm not saying this only because the hourly rate for driving this car is so poor, I need the tips to feed my family. But really, in this country we hold professors in such high regard! Like ex-presidents, right? Why do you think they sent me to pick you up? But to answer your question, sir Professor sir, just look up, on the tops of the buildings in front of us," the driver said.

"I see, oh, I see. I see men with guns. And they are, they are ..."

"Ours! Dragomans security forces. None of these sheikh-brigades and mullah-militias you have to deal with in the other countries. The crazies and funny business that they talk about on, hey!, CNN. Up there are just brave, well-trained boys. All are clean-shaved every morning. Their commander did his training in Florida. Top notch. Those boys up there? You want to know the most important thing about them? They know my car. They know I'm carrying a VIP. So if anyone comes near us—and no one will come near us, trust me—they will take care of it. They will protect. Because if people like you, sir Professor sir, and Bill Clinton, can't come to Dragomans, Dragomans will never be the dream of tomorrow, today," the driver said.

"Thank you, that's very well put," Prin said.

"Sir Professor sir, please, I'm just a simple driver! I'm quoting our new president," the driver said.

"Oh, I see. So, how much longer?" Prin asked.

"You sound like kids in American movie shows! Listen, we are close. And trust me. I do this all the time. We are totally safe. You are totally safe. I have a wife and kids. You think my wife would let me do this if it wasn't safe?" the driver said.

"So, how many children do you have?" Prin asked.

"Five boys!" the driver said.

"That's great. I have four girls," Prin said.

"Four daughters ... hey, that's okay too! You say Canada, I say Allah, it doesn't matter. Children are gifts from God, all over the world. I have two daughters as well!" the driver said.

"Wonderful," Prin said.

"I also have mints and gum up here. My girls need this when they are feeling car sick. So does my wife, when she's pregnant. You want mints?" the driver asked.

"I'm fine, really," Prin said.

He just wanted to get to his hotel. He just wanted to get to his hotel and let Molly know he was safe and to do what was good and right and needed and then go home to his family and to his job, all of it safely in place. And him too, God's good man. Also, he desperately wanted some mints.

27

EVENTUALLY THEY REACHED the complex of government buildings where Prin was to spend the next three days. After passing through a steel gate set in massive cinder-block walls topped with metal spikes, long black gun barrels lolling in between many of them, they drove over a deep-ridged road into a zigzag of security checkpoints, each hemmed in by V-shaped concrete barriers. The barriers were wrapped in images of the President releasing doves and of clasped hands and happy children and women in full hijabs playing soccer while chatting on iPhones.

"We welcome you, Professor, and apologize for these precautions, but we cannot take any chances," said a guard.

"Of course," Prin said.

"Much hotter than ... Canada, yes?" the guard asked.

"Yes, much hotter," Prin said.

"Very good! Justin Trudeau! Drake! Their songs inspire the world! My name is Rafik. If you need anything while you are our guest, remember only one thing: I am here. Also: I am here to protect you. Understood? Now, please wait beside your driver," the guard said.

Prin stepped to the side and Rafik barked at two younger men with significantly less yellow braiding on their uniforms. The two men approached the sedan holding long metal poles affixed with mirrors.

"Those are actually selfie sticks!" the driver said.

He winked dramatically. They'd made it safely. He kept his promise. He had a wife and all those sons, and also the daughters. This guy had daughters. Didn't he hear about the tips?

Prin stepped away from the driver, not wanting all the undulating and smiling and nodding and winking to look like conspiring. His eyebrows hurt from all the squinting he'd been doing in Dragomans daylight. His collar was damp and he could feel beads of sweat running down his cheeks. Much hotter than Canada! Also, his teeth absolutely ached. He must have been clenching his jaw for hours, all the hours since he'd arrived and left the easy foreignness of the terminal—it could have been a luxury-goods mall in Minnesota—for this hard, bright, strange place.

One of the young guards motioned for them to return to their vehicle and so they drove on through the complex, passing identical squat brown buildings set apart by wide, paved roads, stumpy date palms, and elaborate, browning flower gardens. The driver stopped in front of Government of Dragomans Building #4, as the sign read in Arabic, English, and French. It had a giant QR code pasted on one side, and invitations to Like Us on Facebook. There was also a lot of small print in Cyrillic.

The driver wished Prin well, took one of his hands, and pressed into it a whole lot of mints. Then he held out his other open, empty hand. Assuming this was a cultural thing, Prin grabbed it and the two of them sat there, smiling at each other and holding hands as the mints crumbled between them. Eventually Wende came out of the building and gave Prin fifty dollars to give the driver, who praised God and Canada and left.

She wore a buttoned-up shirt and flowing, off-white pants that looked like a dress until she moved her legs. It was kind of weird, like a magic show, how she moved, and it looked like a dress and then like pants, pants, then dress, and also kind of like the necks of swans and Easter lilies. Prin was jet-lagged.

She gave him a firm nod.

"We're being watched right now. We're not married, and we're obviously not family, so no skin-to-skin contact between us, however innocent," she said.

"That's thoughtful of you to let me know, but there's no need, really. Nice to see you and nice to be here. And who's watching us?" Prin asked.

"We're an atheist white woman and a Catholic brown man in a Muslim-majority Middle-Eastern country, Prin. Everyone is watching us," Wende said.

And that's a good thing, he thought, for all of us. He didn't like how smiling and secretive she came across, right away. She certainly didn't smile or sound secretive in UFU meetings, or in VaultTok, or in his living room with his wife and children. So why now? Because she finally could? And could what, exactly?

He wanted to get this over with, right now. Did she really sit in 34C on her flight to Dragomans, or was that information meant to remind him of something? What did she want, really? Who? Not Whom, but really, him? Or was this all in his limp noodle brain? Probably, if he confronted her—Wende, are you trying to break up my marriage?—she'd laugh (and laugh) and show him a picture of her giant Wall Street boyfriend. Of the two of them laid out on a private beach on an island no one had heard of, one of his great white hands basking on one of her legs.

This was business. She needed to do whatever was necessary to make sure he'd come to Dragomans and give his lecture and keep the money coming. And she knew Prin well enough to know that being strung along (and along) could actually be a kind of perfect state of holy fudge for him: just enough to worry about feeling guilty, and not enough to be found guilty, and either way, exactly enough to keep doing whatever it was he was doing. She had done him the greatest mercy, sleeping with another man while they were dating back in graduate school. Otherwise, they might have been sort-of-engaged for all eternity. This was all in his head, 34C.

He followed her into the front hall of the building, which was dark and freezing. Four security guards, each wearing an automatic weapon across his chest, stood positioned in the four far corners of the hall in front of giant air conditioning vents that rippled big banner portraits of the President with the doves and children and soccer moms of Dragomans. There was an empty information desk in the middle of the hall.

"So, there's been a schedule change," Wende said.

"Which is?" Prin asked.

"Good news, actually. It turns out the Minister and some of his staff want to attend your lecture, alongside the students," Wende said.

"Why?" Prin asked.

"I don't know. But what the Minister wants, the Minister gets. So, to accommodate his schedule, the talk has been moved from tomorrow morning to this evening—"

"What time is it right now?" Prin asked.

"Exactly. You need to get some sleep and freshen up so you're ready to give the talk. Because if the Minister's going to be there, and your lecture goes well, this could be really good for us. We need to get you into bed," Wende said.

She curled her lips.

He held his breath.

He held his phone.

He wanted it to buzz with a call from HOME. No he didn't. This was all and only a game. This was all and only business.

"Where's my room, Wende? I want to call my wife and kids, then take a shower, then take a nap, and then get ready to give my lecture. So stop smiling like there's something going on here and tell me where I'm supposed to be and please arrange for someone to get me when it's time to give the lecture," Prin said.

"RAE!"

The Chinese real estate agent popped up from the information desk in the middle of the hall and came over. She took Prin and his bags away.

28

HE SLEPT LIGHTLY, his mind racing and popping and bubbling. When he woke it was as if crepe paper were covering his brain and someone was crinkling it very slowly. Chatting with Molly and the girls had gone badly—the Dragomans Wi-Fi was spotty, and they were on their way to a Milwaukee pool (one of the few that the boys hadn't been banned from yet), and also someone had smeared sunscreen on the phone so his family looked like pixelated mayonnaise.

In the hour before he was to give the lecture, Prin showered, listened to the loud, late afternoon call to prayer blaring out of loudspeakers riveted to all the buildings around them, tried and failed to reach Molly and the girls a few more times, and finally scanned his lecture notes while watching Dragomans TV on a set that had no functioning volume whether by accident or design.

Muted, the channels offered ramrod-spined newsreaders, a documentary about a date farmer, a motorcycle race in Doha, and a cartoon about a young Arabic prince and his wise, portly teacher who took an incredibly long camel ride together through the desert before eventually reaching a metallic city. Prin might have fallen asleep watching the cartoon and dreamt that long camel ride into the future, because when the hotel phone rang like a giggling fire alarm the cartoon had the same young prince smashing his way through an evil liquor store with his wise teacher looking pleased (but also, maybe, winking).

"Prin, are you ready?" Rae asked.

"I am. Will you come get me?" Prin asked.

"I can't. Wende needs me to reserve seats for the Minister and his delegation. We've sent someone," she said.

There was a knock at the door. Prin was escorted to the lecture hall by a tiny, confident woman in ankle-revealing blue jeans, black blazer, and bright turquoise hijab who informed him she'd studied Executive Business Communications at the Resonance School of Homeopathy in Carson City, Nevada. Also, she could not shake his hand.

As they walked to the hall he asked how much further and also, for coffee, many times.

"Thirty seconds away, professor. You really like coffee, huh?" she said.

"Sorry, I'm just a little jet lagged. Also, these cups are really small," he said.

"I'll note that, thanks. The Dragomans Civil Service is committed to continuous client-experience enhancement, so I'll ping our procurement team to look into bigger cups. But don't worry about jet lag, professor. When you feel the energy in the hall, you're going to get all the extra jolt you need. We think this is going to be fantastic. The Minister just came up with the idea yesterday, and it's awesome you accepted!" she said.

"Sorry? Accepted what? I'm prepared to deliver a lecture to an undergraduate seminar on Kafka's *Metamorphosis* and the metamorphosis of sea animals into defining features of modern Canadian literature," Prin said.

"For sure, that sounds really interesting! Hmm. I'm sure it's all going to work out, hashtag Insha'Allah!" she said.

There were a thousand people in the hall. Every civil servant working in the government complex occupied a faded blue seat, each of which was topped by crisp, white headrest towels. Prin knew from watching *Jeopardy* that there was a specific name for them. Whenever he told Molly that one of his articles had been rejected by a journal, he'd come home to dinner in front of the television. She and the girls would cheer him on to Final Jeopardy in their Jesus Lego living room.

He was so, so loved.

Not anti-Communist, not anti-Cossack. What was it?

Waiting in the wings, Prin couldn't tell if there were any students in the crowd, which mostly seemed to be women in various brown business suits and hijabs, and men in brown-on-brown double-breasted jackets. In the front row, alongside the Dragomans professors he'd been meeting over Skype, Prin could see Wende, and Rae, and also the short, shiny Chinese real estate developer who wanted to turn UFU into a retirement condominium. Rae had been profoundly vague about why she was here when Prin had questioned her on the way to his room. Stranger still, why was the developer here?

Meanwhile, the Minister who'd also come to UFU that spring had been replaced by a much younger man, who from just off-stage was vehemently directing his staff to remove the podium and to stop fussing with his black mock-neck shirt. Eventually he ran out in wire-rim glasses and grey sneakers and jeans and the shirt, waving at everyone and thanking them silently and applauding, at which point the crowd began applauding. The words "DRAGOMANS 2.0" crested over massive, crashing waves on the wall behind him.

"So. Friends. I'm not just speaking to you as your new Minister of Education and Strategic Realignment Initiatives. I'm also speaking to you as a fellow influencer and change-maker and thought leader. And IMO, we need to tell our country's story in a different way. Amiright? And why? So we can get to 2.0. And then to 3G. And then eventually, but before anyone else in the Middle East, to 5G. As I said at TED Talk

Albuquerque, we need to inspire each other, and ourselves, and the citizens we serve in our work here. We need to dream and work, and work, and dream a better future. We're going to start by crushing some assumptions about what it means to work in the Dragomans Civil Service. Listen, that's what I want to do, that's why I left my amazing job in Silicon Valley. To be here with all of you, so thank you," the Minister said.

He nodded and the crowd clapped and he made a great show of making them stop clapping. When they did so right away, it seemed to disappoint him.

"Oh, and one more thing ..." the Minister said.

Everyone waited. He waited, too.

"One more thing ..." he said.

This time, his staff began whooping from the wings. The crowd eventually contributed further whooping.

"Thanks! So. Friends. We're not going to change our world by ourselves. We need to listen and learn from inspiring storytellers like our wonderful speaker today, who is inspired, and inspiring. Professor Prin from Toronto is helping us launch a new motivational speaker series that my Ministry is sponsoring as part of Dragomans 2.0. We're calling it ... Drag Racer Talks!"

By now the crowd knew to clap whenever this new young Minister stopped speaking. When their applause ended, the Minister beckoned Prin to join him on stage.

"So. Friends. It's time to hear from our storyteller. He will be speaking to us today about just one word—metamorphosis—and how all of us can transform ourselves and our nation. Many years ago, a passionate and innovative writer, Frank Kafka, absolutely crushed a story about metamorphosis. I remember reading it as a student and being truly inspired. And I want the same for all of you, and for our beloved nation. Dragomans was once a lowly caterpillar. Right now, IMO, it's in a cocoon. In the future, what will it be? Inspired by Kafka and by Professor Prin, I want to believe we will all be drag racers, we will all be butterflies! Friends, I give you Metamorphosis, by Professor Prin!"

The Minister grabbed him and gave him a hug. He didn't let go. He pressed his mouth into Prin's ear.

"We're doing a security sweep of the complex right now. We need to keep these people in this room for sixty minutes. There's nothing to worry about, we're pretty sure. We're just confirming. This is normal around here. So, help us out, bro. Give a long talk that keeps them here and also inspires everybody. My staff will give you an all-clear signal. And we're going to upgrade you to First Class for your flight home!" he said.

"*As-salamu alaykum*. Ladies and gentlemen, who wants to be a butterfly?" Prin asked.

Two hours later, he was still talking. Every single person in the hall, other than Rae, who was taking detailed notes, was asleep. Prin was nearly asleep himself. But he kept going, this time into a summary-review of his earlier point about Martin Buber's I-Thou interpersonal ethic obtaining in asymmetrical terms when it came to understanding Gregor's relationship to his family, pre- *and* post-metamorphosis, and likewise for Ondaatje's English Patient's relationship to his penis when it's both a sleeping and awakened seahorse.

Twenty minutes later, someone nudged one of the Minister's staffers, who in turn sent a text. Within a minute the Minister came from nowhere onto the stage pretending to be an airplane soaring straight into Prin. He mouthed First Class, clapped him on the back, and turned to the audience, which was just waking up and stretching.

"Amazing! Thank you for your words, your wisdom, Professor Prin. So this concludes our first Drag Racer Talk. It's already been posted, and I hope it breaks the internet, right?

You can access it from here, um, soon, but anyway, believe me, people will be watching this everywhere. Now I want to say, before you all return to work, that we need to ask ourselves one question, every day, in these jobs. We need to ask ourselves one question, right now.

"You know the question. You know the answer. So. Friends.

"Who wants to be a butterfly?"

29

"WAY TO GO, team!" said the Chinese real estate developer.

He brought a bucket of champagne to the table where Prin, Wende, and Rae were sitting. Knees were sort-of touching under the table. They were in a Frenchified cafeteria somewhere deep inside another building within the government complex, one that housed the offices of foreign embassies. Now and then, as tonight, the embassies could book the employee cafeteria and, for a short period of time and with no social media allowed and provided the mess was cleaned up before midnight, treat it like home territory.

The French certainly were.

The fluorescent overhead lights had been shut off, and candles and dark-shaded lamps placed in the middle of metal tables covered in creamy white tablecloths. Here and there were little vases of pretty desert flowers and baskets of steaming bread—baguettes flown in from Paris, par-baked and then frozen, then finished in local ovens. The bread was crispy and soft and warm and chewy. The food counter, also covered in creamy white cloth, was set up with bottles of wine and beer and champagne. Two bald, stubbly men took drink orders while a third ran electronic dance music off his laptop. He was dressed in a tri-colour Adidas tracksuit. Twenty or so people, mostly foreign contractors and diplomatic staff, most of them young and bespectacled and thin, were drinking and laughing and strutting to the music.

Knees were definitely touching.

Prin shifted away.

Wende shifted closer.

Prin adjusted his chair again and then reached and clinked his glass with the others before sipping. He was still waiting for an explanation of what they were celebrating, beyond the end of Ramadan, French-embassy style, and also why the Chinese real estate developer was here and why he was so happy about Prin's Kafka lecture.

And how were they a team? Why were they a team?

"Thank you for the champagne and your kind words about my talk … I'm sorry, I still haven't learned your name," Prin said.

"Just call me The Nephew. Everyone does. And even if you don't know who my uncle is, the point is that I have an uncle. An *Uncle* Uncle. Back in Beijing. You know what I mean?" said The Nephew.

"Not exactly," Prin said.

"Probably better for everyone," Wende said.

Prin glared at her while wondering how she was able to keep her shirt that unbuttoned without anything showing. She was smiling at The Nephew, who was re-gelling his hair into great, sharp spikes while surveying the room. Eventually a woman at another table made what technically could be construed as eye contact. He bolted. A moment later, he texted Rae to bring the bucket of champagne to his new table.

"Listen, Wende, something is clearly going on here between you and The Nephew—"

"Are you jealous?" she asked.

"And with the people here in Dragomans, with me and my university somehow caught in the middle of it all. Look, I've left my family behind to be here, and I just gave that exhausting and kind of stressful talk, and I have a responsibility to let my colleagues know whether it makes more sense to open this satellite campus in Dragomans or sell our last building to ... The Nephew. That's what I was told my role was here —"

"It doesn't have to be. It can be more," Wende said.

"I don't want it to be more, Wende! I am not interested. And keep your knees to yourself," Prin said.

"What do you mean? It's a small table," Wende said.

"I am not interested in this," Prin said.

"You know I hate indeterminate pronoun usage. Say it, Prin. Say it and I will leave you alone," Wende said.

"I am not interested in you!" Prin said.

She was about to say something but instead bit her lip. Her eyes, normally blue-gray shiny buttons, grew big and glassy, teary. Never mind the dragon-queen jewellery and sour-lip stuff, Wende looked like a lost little girl just then. He almost wanted to—but she got up from the table and left the room through a side door that had a picture of stairs on it.

Prin sat alone. He drank down his glass of cold, sweet champagne and watched all the happy, drunken bad dancers around him. So she was interested. All these years later. A junior staffer from the French embassy, as sober as an ayatollah, was circulating through the crowd to obtain insurance waiver release consents. All told, Prin was feeling pretty good and true and right. Here was temptation, real and right in his face, and he'd turned it away. All these years later. She had invited all of this, for reasons Prin didn't know or care to know. He was here for work, only he was confused what that meant now. Looking across the cafeteria, Prin tried to get Rae's attention—she'd tell him what was going on with The Nephew. But she was mostly blocked from Prin's view by The Nephew's chunky, Versace'd shoulders, which kept yukking up and down at whatever the woman beside him was saying. Prin got up to leave, waived the need for the waiver and so had to sign a "waiver waiver." He made for the main exit and then his pants buzzed. It was a VaultTok text from Wende.

"Are you sure?"

30

BELOW THE WORDS, an image resolved itself.

He pushed through the side door and she was right there, waiting for him, all her buttons now undone. Her mouth seeking his, she pressed into him, all over him. Prin shook his head away from hers and tried to get past her. He did not try as hard as he could have.

She took him by the hand and walked down the hall to a metal staircase leading to the roof. There was a low humming all around from the air conditioning units, and they could see the rooftops of other buildings in the complex, most of them dotted with men holding cigarettes and big guns. Two approached them right away but then nodded and left, grinning. One gave Prin a green-gloved thumbs-up.

He wanted to kiss her again. No, he wanted to be kissed by her again. No, he wanted to kiss her again. Because, thank God for prostate cancer, what did it matter? Beyond the brain spark at the thought of what she had shown him, what she was offering him, what she was giving him, after all these years, he felt nothing. He could feel nothing. Head, heart, hips: Nothing. At least, he felt nothing in his head and hips.

Technically, this *could* only lead to nothing.

So he kissed her.

She pressed close and moved him with everything she had. Nothing. She ran her hand down his chest, hooked one of her thighs between his legs, and pressed and rubbed. Now her hand pressed down against his hip bone and slid across the front of his pants and searched and searched and stopped. Dropped. She pushed him away and walked to a further, darker part of the roof. Prin followed.

"You're terrible," Wende said.

"What? Why?" Prin said.

"You're terrible. You're a fucking bad person. The last few minutes have made it really, really clear that you're not interested in me, at least not like you used to be. You're only doing this to prove it," Wende said.

"Wait. You think that because I didn't get an, I don't have an … that that means something?" Prin asked.

"For people like us, who live so much in our heads, that's the kind of incontrovertible truth we need, yes. I bet those moron security guards got hard just watching," Wende said.

"Just from seeing you," Prin said.

She put her hands on him again.

"Wende, stop. This isn't going to work. I'm sorry to have to explain this but—"

But what? Why did Prin have to explain this? Maybe she didn't know about the cancer. Molly had told her about something else, in the kitchen. What? It didn't matter. He was invincibly impotent. She was invincibly ignorant. Why not keep things that way?

"But what?" she asked.

"But nothing, I guess. Actually, I'm the one who has questions. Never mind my kissing you back and coming out here. That's something I'm going to have to deal with myself now. I'm a married man. I'm a married man. I'm a—"

"Say it three times and it'll feel true?" she asked.

"Why have you been trying to do this? After all these years, and after the way we ended things, the way you ended things, and with your fancy life now, I'm supposed to believe that you still have feelings for me? Really? I don't. I don't believe that. So what is it? What's the truth? Are you trying to entrap me? Does this have to do with The Nephew?" Prin said.

"Ha. As if I'd need to do that. As if you were really that crucial to what's going on, Prin. It's kind of cute, actually. The Nephew is here in Dragomans with us because we're combining the plans," Wende said.

"Meaning?" he asked.

"Meaning, UFU is going to provide diplomas to Dragomans students in Eldercare Studies. The students will study here and then come to Toronto for internships at the condominium The Nephew is going to build on your campus. Everyone wins," Wende said.

"And how long has this been the plan? Wait, it's been the plan from the beginning, hasn't it! That's why that video we show at the condo lecture has all the young Arab people smiling in the background. Right?" Prin said.

"Does it really matter? You're still going to have a job, and you're going to help some Middle Eastern orphans get educations and jobs in Canada. Do you really care more about that than me?" Wende said.

"Yes! Of course I do!" he said.

"Well, fine. Fuck you, too. And believe me, there's no entrapment going on here. I've been trying to figure something out for a long time, and it's not about you, and it's not about us," Wende said.

"Oh, let me guess … it's about you? That Wende the ice queen bitch-goddess of the wordplay universe can have any man she wants, even the happily married Catholic professor she once dated and cheated on?" Prin said.

He was surprised at how angry it came out. It shouldn't have. He shouldn't have done any of this. What was Prin doing here, all this nothing, when the everything that was his life was somewhere else, waiting for him, smiling?

God had said Go. He'd come. But for this?

"You don't get it, Prin. You never got it," Wende said.

"Please, enlighten me. Actually, don't. I'm going to bed. I'll teach the seminar in the morning and then I'm going home. I'll discuss this with people at the university, and also, yes, I'm going to tell Molly about all of this, *all* of it. And it's going to be awful—you know why? Because what just got wrecked, with you, by you, is real," Prin said.

"Wait, please, just wait. That's it. That's what you don't get," Wende said.

He should have turned and gone. But also, he should have never come up to the roof, gone to the stairs, followed her out of the party, gone with her to the party, left Molly and the girls behind. He should never have come to Dragomans. But God had said Go. He had. He could not deny that any more than he could deny what he'd just done with Wende, what he'd failed to do for Molly. But really, Lord, for this? Also, he should have deleted the picture Wende sent him. But he forgot.

"You know I'm sort of Jewish, right?" Wende said.

"Okay," Prin said.

"So once, when I was a little girl—"

"Seriously? It's going to be one of those?" Prin asked.

"I still remember you telling me about playing peekaboo with candles in church to prove God existed. There's also a passage from *Infinite Jest* I could quote, something about using tennis to prove the existence or non-existence of God. Would that be more acceptable?" Wende asked.

"Just tell the childhood story," Prin said.

"So I never have before. Do you understand? I never have, to anyone," Wende said.

"Okay," Prin said.

"We were driving west one summer. We had a station wagon. My sister and I were allowed to sleep in the big, boxy trunk. Usually, we fought. She was older. I was smarter. I was prettier. I make more money. Way more money. But anyway, we didn't fight when we camped out in the back of the station wagon. We arranged our heads side by side so that we could see the stars while my father drove.

"I remember hearing my mother complain when my father bought coffee and said no to a motel for the night. But we loved it. We got set up all nice and cozy in our sleeping bags and ignored the motor oil and the little red jerrycan smells. We just watched and watched, and it was all disappearing road and the black shapes of tall trees and millions of stars passing through the rear window. Rebekah had her head beside mine. She told me we should pretend we were lying on the backs of carousel horses that had broken free and were flying to the moon. She was my older sister. She was trying to be nice. But even then, and I was probably ten years old, it sounded so childish. I said okay but I wasn't lying on any flying carousel horse. I was thinking about when we would go to my grandparents' house in Newark for Passover. They always recited this really long kind of story and prayer at the same time about the history of the Jewish people and I remember this one time—"

"The Haggadah," Prin said.

"Yes, you're more Catholic and more Jewish than I am, congratulations. Can I continue?"

"Go on," Prin said.

It had been a clue on *Jeopardy*, three rejected-article submissions ago. Molly and the girls. Why was he listening to this unbuttoned woman instead of calling home? Because he couldn't call home. He'd have to tell, or not tell, and he couldn't. Not yet.

"So, God told Abraham: I will make your descendants as many as the stars in the sky. And this one time my grandfather looked over at me and nodded and everyone was looking at me and I could tell I was supposed to say thank you or wow or something. But I didn't. Then my sister leaned over and says 'We're the stars in the sky,' and I thought, no we're not. We're some people sitting around a dining-room table in New Jersey with a lot of candles and it's hot and I'm wearing the crinkly dress I hate and the barrettes in my hair are too tight and I can't eat the bread yet. I looked at my mom and dad and sister and grandparents all looking at me and I thought: How are we stars? How are we anything except a bunch of "me"s? And then it all went away, just like that, Prin."

"What went away?" Prin asked.

"I didn't believe in any of it. In God. The worst was that I didn't even know I didn't believe until that dinner. But whatever, I was a kid, I was hungry and hated my hair and I didn't think much more about it until the next summer, when we were lying there in the trunk of the car and looking up at the sky, at all those stars. They were bright and pretty and I tried to feel something about them, about God and Abraham and me and the rest of us, but they were just things hanging in the air. And we're just things on the ground. And thinking that made me feel very lonely. So I said to my sister, maybe hoping she'd convince me otherwise, 'You don't really think that's us, do you? Like grandpa says God says?'

"Rebekah said: 'Stop it, Wende, or I'll tell mom you're asking weird questions. And I bet she'll tell grandpa. You need to go to sleep now.'

"I waited for her to answer me or tell on me but she just went to sleep.

"And I was so, so alone, Prin, in the back of the car, looking up as my dad drove and drove. I don't know how long this went on for, only that I kept telling myself this is it, this is what it's like."

"What's like?" Prin asked.

"To be us. To be me," Wende said.

"Did it make you want to scream?" Prin asked.

"Why would it?" Wende asked.

"When I was a kid, I once saw a man screaming and screaming and I thought it was because he thought there was nothing out there," Prin said.

He hadn't even told Molly about the man in the hospital parking lot. He had to get away from this.

"So are you saying when you were a kid, you were like me? We—"

"No. I am not like you."

Wende said nothing. She looked away. Then she looked back. Prin worried she was going to put her hands on him again but that was wrong. That wasn't what was on her face. She had taken and tried to take more and yes, he had let her try and still she wanted more from him.

"You're waiting for me to be, what, moved by that story, Wende? Impressed that you were once the youngest atheist in America? Or maybe you want me to feel sorry for you, because apparently you've never had what you think I've always had?" Prin said.

"There it is again! Like when you said something about that screaming man. Your voice was different. Are you saying you don't?" Wende asked.

She looked, for a moment, hopeful. Not just bitten and sad but also just a little hopeful.

"No, Wende. I'm saying it's kind of sad and obvious that you're trying, and I guess you've somewhat succeeded, not in bringing me to disbelief with a story of how you spent your summer vacation losing God, but in getting me to cheat on my wife, because, what? Because somehow this, that, proves there's no God? Is that it, really? Is that all, really?" Prin said.

"Well, if you consider the implications of a religious believer's decision-making—"

"Spare me all the clean, logical little steps in between, which are really just a way to cover your muddy tracks. Enough of this. Let's return, please, to why we're really here in Dragomans. Or is all of this, the work here with UFU and Rae and The Nephew: it wasn't just so you could be proven right about, what, the inconsistencies of your Catholic ex-boyfriend's life? Seriously? All that, all this, just to figure out what everyone else already knows? Please tell me that's not the case. Because otherwise you're trying really hard, Wende, and not for very much," Prin said.

"To you not very much. To me, a lot. Obviously, with this job, with this brain, this body, I can enjoy. And I do. *I do*. I have, for the years since we were together. And I will, for a long time. But when I saw you at that meeting, and then visited your house and saw what you have, all that you have, which is so different than what I have or what I want, I just needed to know," Wende said.

"What?" Prin asked.

"Well, if we can both look up, right now, and one of us sees nothing and the other one sees all of Abraham's descendants, and so I live my way and you live your way, as we have for years, centuries, longer even, does it make a difference in the end? Or are we really just pieces of wired meat, ugly, pretty, fat, thin, whatever, and it just takes the right kind of charge to prove it? I think I proved it," Wende said.

"No. Because of what happens next, for you, and what happens next, for me. You've concluded an experiment. I've broken a bond. But actually, I do think you're right, Wende. We're the same, all of us; you and me as well. But never mind looking up, try looking inside for a moment and tell me what you see, and how that makes you feel. Keep telling yourself it's just a lump of meat sending error messages up and down your circuits. All of this, all these years, you're trying and trying and trying, Wende," Prin said.

"Trying to do what? Answer my question about whether God exists or not?" she asked.

"No. Trying to answer God's question to you, to all of us, each of us, all the time," Prin said.

"You really think it's that simple?" she asked.

"No. But it's there. The question," Prin said.

"Do you have any idea how ridiculous you are?" Wende asked.

"Yeah, that's about it. I think, at some point, we all hear God asking us that question," Prin said.

She left him on the roof. He looked up and around at the Dragomans sky, which, past the white smoke of the various security lights and spotlights, and past the bright green auras floating above all the electric mosque signs, was black and star-filled. Mountain ranges blocked in the horizon, here and there. Which one was it where something, someone involved with the crucifixion had gone? Could he still visit before they left?

Not that it mattered. Visiting or not wouldn't change what Prin believed, what he saw. Because he looked up and around and he still saw darkness shot through with light, true light. Flickering here and there, yes, like the tops of candles hanging down above them, sending down tongues of fire.

Yes, he also had had ridiculous, little-kid ideas about God. And ridiculous little worries, too. But why had his ideas and worries brought him to fullness, and Wende's, to nothing? He could not know the reason why.

And surely this wasn't why God had told him to come to Dragomans. What kind of God would do that? No God.

Just say something—now!

Nothing.

Wende.

Molly.

The girls.

Status naturae lapsae simul ac redemptae: it was fine and well for the convent girls of old Ceylon and for the rest of us. It's always Easter Sunday somewhere. But what Prin also knew, damn but he knew it to his bones, was this: off in the corner of the far heavens hanging above Dragomans, one of those flickering little lights now looked a little smudged.

31

THE NEXT MORNING, Prin went to a meeting room to give his seminar on Kafka to the inaugural class of UFU2. The room was divided down the middle with whiteboards on wheels. Young men sat on one side, young women on the other.

He'd slept very poorly and reached Molly's voicemail enough times in a row to feel like he'd been granted a meta-physical breather before he told her. What an unholy fool he was to think that, because he could feel nothing in technical terms—there had been no movement "down there," as his mother might say (he shuddered that his mother just then came to mind)—he would feel nothing and it would mean nothing. He felt as much for Wende, about Wende, yes. But for Molly? He wanted to get home to her, only he felt like a fish trying to swim after being gutted. After gutting itself. With a dull knife. He'd try calling her again, after the seminar.

"Good morning, ladies and gentlemen," Prin said.

No one on either side responded. Shahad, his local academic host, came over from the women's side of the room.

"Shall I offer a proper introduction?" she asked.

Prin nodded.

Shahad told the twenty-five students crowded into the win-dowless, taupe-walled room that this was a special seminar designed to inaugurate the UFU2 Eldercare Studies program.

Then she introduced their professor for the day, adding that everyone was, of course, already familiar with Professor Prin thanks to the informative and extensive lecture he'd given the day before.

The students themselves didn't look that different from the students he taught at UFU—olive-skinned and phone-addled, though not as showily bored. They looked nervous, most of them swallowing their lips for fear of having to speak. Not all the women were in hijab. Were the others all persecuted Christian orphan girls? What was the name of that girl the Minister had mentioned in Toronto? Shahad returned to the women's side of the room.

"Thank you, Professor Shahad, for that introduction and good morning, ladies and gentlemen!" Prin said.

Still no response.

He looked over at Shahad, who came back to the front and spoke to him quietly.

"Normally, we refer to ladies and gentlemen when we are discussing married people. Do you understand my meaning?" she said.

Prin nodded.

"Good morning, boys and girls!"

"Meh ng," they said.

"So, this morning we're going to discuss Franz Kafka's *Metamorphosis*, as you know, and I'm interested in exploring all the ways the story spoke to you, to your own experiences, which in turn will help establish all the ways that great literature matters to our lives ... and the lives of senior citizens. And while I'll do my best to learn all of your names, just for starters I'm curious, is a student named ... Mariam, here?" Prin said.

Two girls swallowed giggles and briefly turned around in their seats to stare at the girl sitting behind them.

"Hello, Professor," a small voice said.

"Hello, Mariam!" Prin said.

He'd tell Molly about teaching Mariam, too. Not to balance off anything else. That wasn't how this worked. The one didn't cancel out the other. But it mattered, still, on its own. Prin's faith was no longer hiding in the basement with his flat-screen television. Regardless of the rest of what he'd done and failed to do, it was at work right now in the world, the real world, the real, hard world of the Middle East. He flexed his limbs and for a moment he felt like a mustard tree stretching up and throwing shade on all the little mustard seeds around him.

"I should tell you, Mariam, that you're an important part of why we've come to Dragomans. When one of your political leaders came to Toronto earlier this year, he told your story, and it inspired us to help all of you men and wo ... er ... students get educations. But more personally, let me say thank you, Mariam. As a fellow Christian, I have come here in solidarity with you, and I hope, someday, I can live out my faith with as much courage as you do," Prin said.

If only!

No one said anything. Especially Mariam. Shahad was studying her phone.

"Well, I'm sure you all have remarkable stories to tell, about how and why you've signed up for this program. Actually, one of the exercises in the second half of our seminar will be having you write out those stories. But first I'd like us to turn our attention to the situation of Gregor Samsa, the main character in Kafka's story. Now, I appreciate he's not a senior citizen but he's definitely someone who, like a seahorse out of its element and living in Saskatchewan, for instance, needs care and help and is treated poorly by his family and um, has a hard shell, so there's lots of relevance to the program that you're part of, as you can see. Now, I won't rehearse the points I went over in my lecture yesterday; I'd like to hear from you. So, what did you think of the story?" Prin said.

There was no response. Prin felt better. Other than the dividing wall in the middle of the class, this was no different than teaching in Toronto. He made a well-practiced, mock-surprised face.

"Okay, everyone, confession time. Who didn't complete their readings for today's class?" he asked.

No one raised a hand.

"So all of you read the story?" Prin asked.

Everyone nodded.

"This is one of the most original and provocative works of literature of the modern age. And none of you have anything to say about it?" Prin said.

Some time passed.

Much time passed.

Finally, a young man raised his hand. He was wearing a T-shirt that read WE FOUND THE WEAPONS OF MASS DESTRUCTION, with arrows pointing at his biceps.

"May I ask you a question, Sir Professor?" he said.

"Of course. You can ask me anything. Kafka would want it that way," Prin said.

"Who?"

"So, are there any questions about the readings?" Prin asked.

No one spoke.

"Are there any questions, at all?" Prin asked.

"How cold does it get in the winter? In Canada, I mean," asked THE WEAPONS OF MASS DESTRUCTION.

"Well, ah, certainly it's cold, much colder than here, I'm sure. But really, you can look that up online," Prin said.

Shahad looked up from her phone and gave him a discreet but very negative nod.

She hadn't even been wearing sour apple on her lips. He'd come all this way and scuffed up his life, for questions about the weather?

164

"Really, that's the only question you have?" Prin asked.

Another hand went up. Mariam's. Mariam!

"Yes, Mariam?" Prin said.

"When we come to Canada, how long do we have to wash and clean the old people before we get our degrees and take the other jobs? And how many relations are allowed to come with us?" she asked.

"Those are, well, important questions, and I'm sorry but I can't offer specific answers," Prin said.

Both sides of the classroom sagged.

"But I wonder if we might look at a moment in the *Metamorphoses* where Gregor's family has to wash and clean him, just to get another perspective."

Further sagging.

"How would that sound, Mariam?" Prin asked.

"Sir, apologies, but it's Miriam! Miriam, not MAAriam! Sir, sorry, but you make her name sound like you're stepping on a duck. MAAriam! MAAriam!" said one of the other students.

"Also, Sir, Mariam's not a Christian!" said the girl sitting beside her.

"Oh, my apologies, I didn't realize you were Muslim, Mariam," Prin said.

"Sir, she's not! She's Mandaean," said the same girl.

"Haram!" a boy in the back called over the whiteboards.

"Mushrikun!" called out another.

Prin looked over to Shahad, who was still studying her phone.

"Oh, okay, thank you. I'm not familiar with the Mandaean faith," Prin said.

He looked at Miriam.

She was clearly not interested in familiarizing him with the Mandaean faith. The girl beside her spoke rapidly, in a whisper, in Arabic. Then she turned back to Prin.

"Sir, they, how to say, worship the John the Baptist. Isn't that how you put it?" said the same girl.

Mariam nodded.

"Haram!"

"And most of you have moved to Michigan, no? How many of you are left?" asked the same girl.

"Haram!"

"Mushrikun!"

"Forty," said Mariam.

"Haram!"

32

"SO. YOU SURVIVED," said Wende.

"Indeed," said Prin.

It was an hour after the seminar had finished. They were alone in a room with stacks of paper that Prin was supposed to sign on behalf of UFU, confirming the educational partnership with this new school in Dragomans.

"When Shahad brought in these documents, she told me what happened in the seminar, with the students. From what she said, I think you did well, all things considered. Also, I think, Prin, to be fair, you were a convenient target for a lot that had nothing to do with you," Wende said.

"Are we talking about this morning's seminar with the students, or last night on the roof?" Prin asked.

"Hi team! Hope I'm not interrupting anything, right? And are we all signed up? Time to go back to Toronto and sell baby, sell, yeah?" asked The Nephew.

Despite the windowlessness of the room and the general brown aura of Dragomans buildings, The Nephew was wearing sunglasses. And what was that in his voice, when he mentioned interrupting them? Had he seen Prin chase after Wende last night? Had Rae? She was now standing beside The Nephew with a blank expression on her face, holding a tray of date smoothies. Prin nodded at her, but she didn't nod back. She was willing to sell condos and kidneys to get her family back together. He ran after other women who texted him chest shots.

"Sorry, Nephew, but like I said to Wende, last night—"

"Yes you did! You di-id!" said The Nephew.

"I explained to her that regardless of what you think the plan may be, I have a responsibility to report to my colleagues at the university on two different options for our future. This is what we all agreed to, in the beginning of all of this, Prin said.

"And now that you've given your talks to the old people in Toronto, and met the young people here, isn't it obvious what we should do? We put this and this together and boom! There's lots of money and people going in lots of better places than where they are now. Everybody wins!" said The Nephew.

He kept making exploding motions with his hands.

"You're likely right, Nephew, but—"

"Fuck buts," said The Nephew.

"Sorry, what?" Prin said.

The Nephew moved in much closer to Prin. He was very thick through the arms and shoulders and had veins, serious veins, pulsing up and down along his neck. His meaty hands were turning into, what, fists?

Seriously?

Prin grinned. He was a university professor! He had mandatory travel insurance! This was a curriculum meeting, not some Asian crime show.

"I'm sorry, Nephew, but are you, a real estate developer, trying to intimidate me into signing something related to university course offerings? That's a bit ridiculous, isn't it? I'd add, also, that you're doing this in front of two witnesses," Prin asked.

But when he looked around, Wende and Rae were gone.

Prin stopped grinning.

"What witnesses?" The Nephew asked.

He probably couldn't get past him and out the door. They were deep inside a dimly lit office building where very few people appeared to work other than the guards positioned in front of the foyer air conditioners.

"What intimidation? Nothing like that's going on, bro!" said The Nephew.

"Then what is going on here? I am not—"

"Yes you are. You are. Hey! Stop looking worried! Nothing is going on, okay? I'm sorry you think that. We're on the same team, remember? There's no reason to be worried. This is also about more than us, Professor," The Nephew said.

"Right, exactly. For instance, one of the students was asking about her academic standing here versus Toronto, as this relates to—"

"Obviously, we both do well, and so do the other professors. All the good stuff. None of the bad stuff. Just sign, okay?" said The Nephew.

"Sorry, but I'm not sure about this," Prin said.

"About what? You are going to break the internet with good news! Hashtag Professor saves the day! Also, so does Wende, and I know you care about that, right? Right? Don't think I didn't see you follow her out last night. Don't think the rooftop is camera-free. Don't think I can't access those cameras. But also, Mr. Married Man, Mr. Family Man, think about this: If this deal works out, Rae gets to bring her family over and stop that other stuff she does for money. I know she told you about it. Right?" said The Nephew.

"You did," said Prin.

Of course there were cameras on the rooftop. But why would The Nephew have access to government security footage?

He must be bluffing.

Wasn't he just bluffing?

Or why not just sign and get out of here?

He had to tell her. He would tell her. He could sign the papers and then there would be nothing else but to go to his room and call and tell her.

"Anyways, I don't know what you see around town, but do you know how many Russian strippers I've met in Toronto with scars near their kidneys? Sure, they call them birthmarks and scars from where the babies came out. They have to. But they're lying, the poor, sexy girls. That's awful stuff. Really bad. Right?" said The Nephew.

"This is not the way the meeting was supposed to go," said Prin.

"Lots of things don't go the way they are supposed to go. Just ask Rae. We don't want her doing that kidney stuff anymore, do we? We want her to have a nice life like you have, with your wife and your kids. All you have to do is sign. And trust me, whatever's going on with you and Wende is none of my business, unless it affects my business. Understood?"

"You didn't see anything. Because nothing—"

"Hey, what happens in Dragomans stays in Vegas. You know what I mean? Unless it's uploaded to YouTube. But forget worrying about that. Just sign. Or don't. And then what you'll be worrying about won't be YouTube. It'll be my Uncle. Are you?"

"YouTube?"

"Please, don't even think about my Uncle right now! Oh no, are you? Please, don't believe what you read about him online. It's all exaggeration. And it's nothing compared to what these people here, in this place, do to people who get in their way. Who don't sign. Remember that Osama bin Zuckerberg who introduced you for your lecture? *His father's done things so bad, he can't even visit North Korea,*" said The Nephew.

"You would email my wife?" Prin asked.

"Is that what's worrying you? Your wife and your four daughters, and my Uncle? Just sign and don't worry about it," said The Nephew.

"I wasn't thinking about that at all, actually. I was asking what you said about last night; wait, what did you just say about my daughters?" asked Prin.

"Molly and the girls—what is it again? Maisie, Chiara, Philo-something, and what's the fourth one's name?" asked The Nephew.

Pippa.

"All of you living in that nice little house on Candlewick Avenue. You and Molly sleeping in the front bedroom, the girls in bunk beds in the back bedroom ..."

Prin signed.

33

HE FORCED DOWN celebratory date smoothies with Rae and Wende and The Nephew and then went back to his room to pack. Their flight was that night. Finally, Prin's cell coverage returned. His phone buzzed and pulsed again and again. He had thirty-two new messages. How did she know already?

But she didn't. Not yet. He would tell her, soon. The thirty-two messages were from his parents. His Drag Racer lecture had been posted to YouTube and someone had forwarded it to his parents, who now knew he wasn't in Milwaukee; he was in the Middle East.

Seventeen of the messages were from Lizzie, sixteen of which were incoherent sobs with a pug barking in the background. The other was from her husband, Kareem. He told Prin that if he met anyone who wanted to harm him—though Islam is a religion of peace, so he probably wouldn't meet anyone who wanted to harm him, but just in case—that he should say *La illah ila Allah, Muhammad Rasul Allah*. Kareem's translation: "Don't worry, brother, we're on the same team!" At least, that's what Prin thought he heard as Kareem tried to speak over Lizzie's sobbing and the pug.

Kingsley had left fifteen voicemails. The first was addressed to Prin. The rest were addressed to his kidnappers. To Prin, Kingsley asked why he was risking his life and ruining the lives of his wife and children by growing a beard and giving a lecture in the Middle East, "the suicide-bomber-exploding-toilet-bowl-of-the-world." If Prin survived and came back to Toronto, he was grounded for a year. Finally, Kingsley was taking back the flat-screen television he'd given Prin as a house-warming present years before, because he was sure Prin never watched it or let his children watch it, which, in the twenty-first century, is like child abuse. Also, Kingsley obviously had to go to Sri Lanka to get a new wife now.

This last piece of information felt very, very tacked on.

The other fourteen messages from Kingsley were a rotating combination of insult rants directed at his son's terrorist kidnappers, offers of guaranteed future casino winnings in exchange for Prin's release, and hoarse begging for his son to be spared. In the final message, Kingsley took it all back, then offered it all again, and then just said, "Please, he's my son, please," before hanging up, poorly, and at length.

Prin was overcome for a moment with the nose-tingling, eye-watering sense of just how much his parents loved him, how madly. By the time he'd finished listening to the messages, a new one had come through. Prin listened. It was from Molly! Only it wasn't Molly. It was Pippa, their youngest.

"Hi Dad. Where are you? I miss you, Dad. I want to show you my mosquito bites and see your hotel room. When are you coming home? Dad isn't answering, Mom. Can I play a song on your phone?"

He heard Molly in the background. His heart was already smashing around in his chest just to hear the sweet, slurry sound of Pippa's little voice. Hearing Molly in the background, knowing she was awake right now, standing in the middle of Milwaukee, their children all around her ... now was the time to call. His heart was pulling, thrashing, trying to go deep caught at the end of a line. This was the time he *could* call, but what would that do to her, just then, there with them all around her? Out of nowhere—worse still, if she wasn't surprised—what a car wreck he'd be giving her. What if she were driving, in fact?

Now that there was no chance of her being emailed about it first, what risk was there in waiting until he got home and could tell her in person, in their bedroom, with lots of contextualization and reports on subsequent reflections and prayers, with the children asleep down the hall, with the downstairs couch awaiting him?

Yes, that's all it would take—a good and full and thoughtful accounting, and then days, weeks, even months of sleeping on the couch. He could hide sober and scouring spiritual reading under the cushions—hardcovers that he'd sleep on for added mortification.

He paced around his room, thinking it through, careful not to look to his left when he passed by the mirror.

He called Molly.

"Hi Prin! Girls, it's Dad!" she said.

"Molly, can we talk?" he asked.

But she didn't hear him. There was too much cheering and pleading for the phone. He ended up speaking with each of his daughters, and then with a couple of nieces and nephews. Molly thanked him from the background—chatting with the kids gave her enough time to finish folding laundry.

He put them on speakerphone so he could look up the metaphysical implications of failing to do penance for a mortal sin. The screen wouldn't respond to his sweaty prompts. It just smudged and smudged.

Roasting in Hell for eternity, an eternity of being punished for trying and failing to look up rules for penance because the screen of your phone is soaked in sweat because you're roasting in Hell.

But God, he intended to tell her!

He just needed, well, the right setting.

It could be the first night he returned home, or maybe the second because of the jet lag, or the third because he volunteered to pick up the house while she went to bed early for a change.

Or the fourth night, the fifth ... and on and on it could go until they were mild old people and by then wouldn't he be risking Dante territory for her?

Prin looked in the mirror. He looked right back. They both nodded. But just before one looked away, the other said hold on, come closer, can you hear me?

What are you thinking?

What am I saying?

"Bullshit," Prin said.

"Daddy? What did you just say?" one of his daughters asked.

"Nothing, sorry. What were you saying?" Prin asked.

"Daddy, there's a skunk with three legs living in Grandma's backyard!"

"No Daddy, it's a skunk with four legs. One of them is disabled. And I think it lives under the neighbour's porch."

"Daddy, do you know what would have been a good way to capture the skunk? First, put glue on the pavement—"

"You can't put glue on pavement!"

"LET ME TELL! IT'S MY WAY TO GET THE SKUNK! First, glue on the pavement and then get a real gun from the cousins and shoot the skunk in a box and then put a box on it. But we don't have a real gun. And if someone gets hurt, we need to call the ambalance."

"Portland's pet shark died!"

"THAT'S MY STORY TO TELL DADDY! And it's not true. She made it up."

"Daddy, can you bring us Tic Tacs? Do they have Muslimic Tic Tacs?"

"Mommy said we're allowed to sleep in our sleeping bags until you get home!"

"Daddy, our skunk has only three legs. The fourth is disabled, like when Pippa tries to put the password into Mommy's phone."

"I know her password! It's a secret from all of you! Mummy only told *me*, right Daddy? Daddy, when are you coming home?"

"Alright girls, enough! Now it's my turn to talk to Daddy," Molly said.

There came a great gnashing, pleading, and rustling on the line. Finally, she had him to himself.

"How was the lecture? How are things going? We miss you! I miss you. You're flying home tonight, right?" she said.

"Yes, we're leaving for the airport in a bit," Prin said.

"And everything has gone well?" Molly asked.

"Molly, I, I ..."

"Yes? What is it, dear? Is everything okay? You're coming home soon!" she said.

"I kissed Wende."

"..."

"Hello? Are you there? Molly? Are you there?" Prin said. She was not.

34

HE RODE BY himself to the airport. Rae, Wende, and The Nephew had no interest in making a side trip to visit the famous chapel in the mountains from Biblical times. Neither did Prin. He wanted to go there, now, because it was the only functioning church left in the country.

Two hours after leaving the government complex, Prin and his driver, a new one, had made it out of the old city and onto the blunt, bland road that ran to the airport. They exited at a juncture between the blast walls that Prin hadn't noticed on the way into the old city. They went through set after set of security checkpoints until they were cleared to proceed along a thin, dusty road towards a large, orangey-looking mountain, all hard and jagged-edged. There were no green daubs of trees or peaky snowcaps or even clouds floating by. This was all and only mountain.

This driver had been quiet throughout the drive, leaving Prin with his thoughts. Which was, which were, awful.

Molly wasn't taking his calls.

He needed to kneel down.

He needed to kneel down and name what he had done. The video cameras on the rooftop would show nothing. The nothing of two bodies pressed together for a minute, maybe two. They wouldn't show his lusting, leaking, suppurating heart.

How long? How long, Lord, had he been wanting and not-wanting something with Wende? But in fact it didn't matter that it was Wende. This wasn't about Wende. What mattered was that somewhere inside that dented thing, his heart, he did not want Molly.

For how long? How long, Lord?

And how to tell that? Who could hear that and let him go on? He had to kneel.

"First time to see *Kaneesat al-Himar al-Muqaddas?*" the driver said.

"Is that the name of the place where we're going?" asked Prin.

"Is what we call it here," said the driver.

"And what's the translation, into English?" asked Prin.

"Hard to put in English," said the driver.

"Give it a try," said Prin.

"Okay. My English is not so good when it's not stuff about driving, okay? But, *Kaneesat al-Himar al-Muqaddas*, I think it would be something like the Church of the Holy Ass," said the driver.

"So then, okay, well, how did this figure in the crucifixion? Do you know? Perhaps it's named for the donkey that brought Christ into Jerusalem for Passover?" asked Prin.

"Yes. Okay. Very holy place for Christians. Tremendously holy, as you Americans say. But not donkey. I mean, you know—"

"Oh. I'm sure there's something a little lost in the translation. Also, I'm Canadian," said Prin.

"Okay," said the driver.

They didn't speak for the rest of the trip. Theirs was the only vehicle going in to the site. Now and then a tour bus or shuttle came at them from the opposite side, and each driver would pull halfway onto the sand-coloured gravel shoulder so both could pass at the same time, waving. On either side of this narrow road it was all rubble and flatness broken up here and there by clumps of yellow-green shrub and metal-box houses and spindly goats. There was laundry—bedsheets? Tunics? Tablecloths? Was there any point in bringing Molly something from Dragomans?—hanging flat on lines in the hot, dead air. He could even make out the smudge marks of last night's fires in a few places. Prin saw no people at all. He needed to kneel down and he needed Molly to answer the phone, but shouldn't this worry him, too?

Were they all at work?

Or were they also hiding?

From what?

At the foot of the mountain, the van came under sudden shade and they turned off into a parking area half-full of other vans. Prin's driver made it clear he was going to sit on a bench under a clump of mopey midget palm trees and play games on his phone until Prin returned from the chapel. And so Prin walked ahead, alone, breaching the Biblical mountain and wishing his wife would answer the phone.

He tried her again. In vain.

This whole trip—had it been in vain? Had it been about his vanity? Pride? Lust?

He knew others would laugh at this suffering, at what he was treating as adultery, what Molly was treating as adultery. What bare, numb lives they must have. Not the lives he and Molly had been given, had given each other, were trying and trying and trying to give their girls.

He swallowed dry and hard at the idea of his daughters asking him what he'd done on his trip. Were the people nice? Did he make any new friends?

Someone emerged from the shadows wearing a red chequered kaffiyeh. His arms were full of water bottles for thirsty sir. Prin waved him away and made for the church. His wife would not answer the phone. He needed to kneel down and tell and tell and tell and wait in the candle flicker to hear something, someone, tell him he should, please God, what?

Prin walked forward.

Here, sun and shadow were at odds in close quarters. The sun lit up long, jagged ruts and cuts, runnels that had gone dry along the mountainside. A few hundred paces away and more in shadow than sun sat a small, squat church carved into the mountain base where the cleft closed. Its facade was a mish-mash of bas-relief Eastern domes and classical columns beneath a cross that looked like two big dry biscuits laid one upon the other at ninety degrees. Prin pinched his phone's screen to get an extreme close-up of the cross.

"STOP!" said a man.

Not just a man, a monk.

He was big, broad, and dressed in black and wore a hammer-thick silver cross under his big bird's nest of a beard. He was standing just ahead, arms crossed, beside where the line to get into the church began.

God's very own bouncer.

The monk pointed to a sign nailed into the rock wall behind him.

"We must preserve the holiness of this site. NO pictures!" it read in various languages.

He then jerked his thumb to the side, to a gift stall staffed by two vacant-faced women in black kerchiefs.

"Buy pictures there when you leave," he said.

"NO!" said another monk, who emerged from the other side of the line. He was as barrelled and grim-faced and nest-bearded, only he wore a heavy silver cross on a jute-coloured cassock.

"Buy pictures *there* when you leave," he said.

He pointed to another little gift stall, just up from the first one. It was staffed by two vacant-faced women wearing jute-coloured kerchiefs.

Prin nodded at both monks, who were now glaring at each other, and slipped his phone into his pocket. He walked on, joining other pilgrims lined up to enter the chapel. Directly in front of him was a large group of Africans, all of whom were dressed in bright blue jumpsuits and carried white umbrellas. Two turned, smiled, and nodded at him, sweat beading down their faces. They leaned in and Prin smelled floral cologne and Lux soap.

They wore nametags that read I'M BLESSED BRUCE and I'M BLESSED ROY.

"Hello," Prin said.

"BLESSED! And blessings to you!" said Bruce.

"BLESSED! and blessings to you!" said Roy.

"Thank you," said Prin.

"Is this your first time visiting the Holy Church?" I'M BLESSED BRUCE asked him.

"Yes. Can you explain why the church is called, according to my driver's English translation—" asked Prin.

"Hello boss! You have questions? You would definitely like a tour guide! I spent a day with Harrison Ford when they filmed an *Indiana Jones* here! Han Solo! You would like to skip the line! Don't worry, I'm government-certified and can arrange everything, totally for free. No cost at all. Guaranteed. 110 percent. I just want to practice my English! Come with me! Are you from England? Manchester U! Princess Kate! Princess Meghan!"

A loud, small, smiling man had appeared out of nowhere. He was bony and a little gristly, his clothes old and threadbare; his sandals mere notions of footwear. He wore a lot of lanyards, all of which appeared to hold formal credentials of one kind or another.

"Can you tell me why this church has this name?" Prin asked.

"Of course! I can explain everything!" the guide said.

He took Prin's wrist very gently. Then he closed his grip and pulled a little. The Africans watched, smiling beatifically and nodding along with the conversation.

"Please, just come with me," the guide said.

"Blessings to you and to you," Prin said.

The Africans stopped smiling when Prin stepped out of line and passed them and the rest of their group, the guide leading the way in a righteous and barking manner as if he were trying to get Princess Diana past all the photographers to her car. But when they emerged near the front of the line, he didn't take Prin directly into the church. Instead, he took him to the fur-thest giant stone door from the small, dark entrance. He did a thing with his neck, cleared his throat, and began.

"Welcome to the Church of the Holy Seat, which is one of the most important historical sites in all of the world and a source of greatest national pride in Dragomans, regardless of your race, religion, or sexual orient nations, except North Korea. As to why this church is of greatest significance, there are several reasons, many dating back centuries and even millennium falcon. Sorry, Star Wars joke. I made it with Harrison Ford and he loved it. Now, to begin our exploration, I would like to read the following statement by our President regarding the importance of preserv-ing our innovative heritage. He declares—"

"Sorry, but I have to catch a flight. Is there a pamphlet or something I can look at? And can we go in?" Prin said.

The guide nodded. Why wouldn't anyone let him give this speech? His wife and mother thought it was excellent. At least, his mother did.

"Of course we can still go in. But please understand, with a wife and children to support, and also a mother, if I can't practice my English on you, there's need for a small fee for me to arrange everything," said the guide.

"What if I don't pay?" asked Prin.

"No problem, boss. Nice to meet you, enjoy your visit to the church and the rest of your time here in beautiful Dragomans. Like us on the Facebook, and please tell all your friends in English to visit Dragomans. Now, sir, please be pleased to return to the line. And I am required to call the brother over there if you do not respect the rules," said the guide.

He shrugged and grandly bowed and extended his arm to show Prin the way back. Prin looked at the beefy monk with his crossed arms and didn't want him called over. He looked at the line. The Africans hadn't moved yet, and another tour group had arrived. They were sullen white people, glowering men in denim and fanny packs and pouty women with shotgun makeup faces and black rocker booties and matching purses with lots of gold crosses and dingles dandling from them.

They were either Russian or Polish.

He looked down. He saw a rock move. It was a baby lizard, round and coloured like a rock. He moved his toe towards it and it was gone.

"How much?" Prin asked.

"Please, I can't say. That is not our way here. Whatever you can offer, I will gladly accept, and then I will arrange everything," the guide said.

Prin took out his wallet.

"My wife just had a new baby ... jaundice!" the tour guide said.

Prin gave him a twenty-dollar bill and didn't wince, not particularly, when the tour guide looked shocked. He beamed to himself, then at Prin before running off to the gift stalls and returning with two poorly photocopied pamphlets. They were histories of the church, exact copies of each other, with certain words underlined or crossed out in one, and the opposite set underlined and crossed out in the other.

"And now, distinguished, honoured guest, welcome to the Church of the Holy Seat," the guide said.

Perhaps he'd been mishearing the entire time. If this was the Church of the Holy See, then did it have some special papal significance dating to St. Peter? Or perhaps it was a Holy Sea —somewhere else Christ had walked on water, in one of the apocryphal Gospels?

Holding the pamphlets, Prin followed the guide inside. He felt a little like a running back moving behind a blocker as the guide pushed through the people colliding everywhere in the back of the church. Eventually, they were organized into two sort-of line-ups to approach the holy site located behind the main altar.

According to two millennia of pious tradition, the church was founded on the site where a young man, who had been a follower of Jesus, came after escaping the Garden of Gethsemane during Christ's arrest. As the Gospel of Mark recounted, the young man left the Garden so fast he dropped his loincloth, which was all he was wearing. According to pious tradition, naked the young man ran and ran and ran, out of Jerusalem and across Egypt, across the desert of Lehabim, and finally into Dragomans. Naked and terrified, he finally reached a cleft in a great mountain, where he found a rock ledge, sat down, and wept. He wept knowing he had abandoned his Lord in His time of trial, and knowing what had happened to Christ while he ran away, knowing what God had allowed to happen to His Only Son for the sake of all weeping fleeing terrified humanity. And according to pious tradition, this nameless and naked young man wept so much the rock ledge beneath him softened from all of his tears and took on the shape of his seated body (buttocks), which remained there until his death. Four centuries later, all that remained of this young man was a mound of grey dust resting upon the ledge in the cleft of the mountain.

Now one day, two men who were part of a new order of desert monks happened to be travelling through these mountains seeking a spot for the monastery they planned to found together. They came to this cleft and one of them (as to which one, the pamphlets emphatically differed) swept this grey dust off the ledge before sitting down to rest and see whether from this ledge he could observe the greatness of God and contemplate it for the rest of his days. Upon sweeping away the dust and sitting down, the monk discovered this holy seat, imprinted with the mark of the naked young man of Mark's Gospel (buttocks) who had fled from his Lord's side and wept unto his own death, having abandoned his God and feeling terrified that his God would abandon him. But God did not. Instead, God led this pious monk (again, as to which one, the pamphlets emphatically differed) to the place where the naked young man had stopped running and sat down. And because both monks claimed for the rest of their lives to have been the first to have swept away the dust and discovered the imprint of the holy seat and sat there, and because each likewise claimed to have recovered all the young man's ashes and kept them in a sacred urn, two rival orders of monks were founded that day. And for sixteen centuries since, these orders had shared custody of the church built around the Holy Seat.

35

IT WAS A small, dark place, and the air was close with many bodies and drying, dying flowers and guttering candles. What natural light there was came in through a series of bar-shaped openings cut into the main façade of the church. These threw just enough light down onto the floor to reveal a blue-white spread of mosaic tiles that occupied the centre of the church's floor, at the beginning of the nave. Many tiles were missing, all were faded, but Prin could still make out the image of a naked young man artfully concealed, his head down, one hand resting upon his brow as he sat on stone and sobbed.

Very few people were actually praying before the altar on the two or three little benches set up there. Instead, everyone was lined up along the aisles, waiting for their chance to venerate the Holy Seat and in the meantime leaving flowers and lighting candles at all the little apse shrines available to them along the way.

But now that he was in a church and could at last kneel down, Prin didn't know what to pray for.

No, that wasn't it.

He knew all and only what he wanted to pray for—for Molly, and also for a time machine, to take him back just a day. Because he was certain that, given the chance, he would have just deleted that picture Wende had sent him while he was sitting at that table in the French embassy cafeteria and then gone to his room and called home.

He thought again of those little metal houses he'd seen on his way to the chapel. Where were those people? Were they hiding? Were they running away? There were so many such people now, then, always, including Prin, including the naked young man of the Gospel. But some didn't hide or run away. A little Spanish girl singing the *Magnificat* before the conquering Moors. As a boy, Prin had read about her in a comic book saint's life. Did she really keep singing after they chopped her head off? Until her voice was muffled by the great beating of the pure white doves escaping from her open neck?

There were so many such saints' lives—crazy holy men and women, boiled and split and scalped, left to broil in the belly of a giant metal pagan pig god and hammered against this spiked wall, daggered upon the floor of that lion-filled chamber, and in and through it all the saints are still singing, never denying, always praising God. Some had been seen by hundreds looking beatific, their brown eyes turned Virgin blue in Midland, Ontario, or while kneeling before floating golden chalices bearing the bloody heart of Christ in Hackeborn, in Helfta, in Haifa. And when, whether right away or at long last, these saints died and went to the greater reward, people came to these places, cross-covered dovecotes in Andalusia and bum-shaped stone ledges in Dragomans, and prayed there, waited there with candles and flowers until those in charge caught up and built a church.

A chord pulled and began trilling in an arc that ran from his heart to his mind. He strained his ears in vain for a matching voice. But then he knew he didn't need it, here.

In the very place where Prin now was, as he saw just before he passed behind the altar to the site of the Holy Seat itself, there hung a simple bronze chain that came down and down and down from the centre-point of the cracked, vaulted ceiling. The chain held an iron mesh basket in which sat a small red amber globe, in which sat a thick round candle. And yes, it was flickering, the candle was always flickering, whether in the suburban church of his childhood or the New Year's Day church of his dark zoo midlife or right here and now in Dragomans, because this red amber globe, every such globe, hung before small stone vaults set into altars inlaid with old, flaking gold.

And in all of these vaults, in this vault before him, there was a simple golden chalice, within which rested the thin, encircled body of Christ.

Rests.

But then the trilling chord went slack. He could have felt such fullness down the street from his house. With his wife and children beside him. Why did it have to be here, like this, after *that?*

Prin wanted to throw himself against the vault. He had betrayed Molly and their girls and another. You. You brought me here. For this? To this? To betray them? To betray what You want of me, for me? What kind of God? No God would. No God.

No.

No?

No.

There was still no denying. The stars above were smudged, but they remained. Prin still wanted to be shattered, warmed, found, kept, filled, spared, caught and released, explicated, expiated, saved, and sent home.

He wanted to go home.

He dropped down upon the cracked mosaic floor, closing his eyes to say something, anything, to ask for something, anything, to hear something, anything. Did he? Was it? Was it yes, that he felt God pulling him here and not for him, not for him not only for him, but for all of these other people, for Molly and the girls, even, yes for W— but then the guide, who was hopeful of getting a second twenty-dollar bill on the way out, grabbed him under the armpits and heaved him forward so they could hurry up and get to the front of the line.

He was, in fact, second in line on the black robe side. On the other side was a matching line controlled by the jute monks. The area itself, which was located in a large apse behind the main altar, was very tight. The ceiling sloped down dramatically, and the air was thick and shared by all the people crammed in there along the ambulatory, waiting their turn to venerate the Holy Seat.

The arrangement, going back centuries, was for the two orders to alternate visitors approaching the Holy Seat itself, one at a time. In the meantime, those closest to the front of each line could contemplate flanking smaller shrines, each of which held, behind thick, cloudy glass, a bejewelled urn said to contain the true ashes of the absconded and unnamed young disciple of Jesus. The shrines themselves were drenched in generations of candle wax and dry flowers and memorial cards for the beloved dead.

"Front of the line, here you go!" the tour guide said.

He was shushed by the jute monk managing the line on the far side of the Holy Seat. The black monk standing near Prin shushed back his counterpart, who squared up and glared. The monks gestured back and forth, at their chests and crosses and lineups, and then the jute monk pointed violently at the young man in front of Prin, who was thin and troubled-looking. His hands held forth in supplication, he was approaching the Holy Seat on his knees, very slowly.

The jute monk crossed to the black monk's side and pushed the young man's shoulder to get him to hurry up so the next pilgrim, the jute monk's pilgrim, could have his turn. The black monk didn't like this at all.

"Laqad han dawruna!"

"Lo! Laqad han dawruna!"

"*Kadhaab!*"

"*Alyahudi!*"

They bumped back and forth, chest to chest, umpire and manager, crosses clinking like nails being hammered while they accused each other of lies and deceits that went back hours and days and days and centuries. The whole time the young man kept inching along on his knees. Prin saw the person next in line on the jute side whisper to his buddy. He was a long young man in white patterned shorts and a LeBron James jersey. Prin saw him take a long steel cylinder out from behind him.

Oh God! A rifle!

Oh no! A selfie stick!

He stole ahead and sat down in the Holy Seat. He struck a manspreading pose that revealed the pattern on his shorts was actually a blonde woman in a bikini who stretched across his hips. He held the selfie stick in front of him, grinned, and snapped away.

The monks stopped fighting and together chased the young man off the Holy Seat and out of the church. The young man's friend followed after them, laughing and recording it all with his phone. With the monk gone, the tour guide took Prin by the arm, stepped over the kneeling man still making his way forward, and pushed him towards the Holy Seat, where Prin got down on his knees.

Not knowing what else to do, and really not liking the theological implications of kissing this particular piece of sacred space, he placed a hand on the smooth, slight indenture in the stone and nearly demanded to know why God had told him to come here and then gone silent. Instead, he prayed that he be given the courage and grace never to run away from God. Again.

36

PRIN SAW THE sacrilegious manspreader again a few hours later, in the Duty-Free Shop at the Dragomans airport. The young man and his friend were deliberating between towering bottles of rum. Prin took a step towards them. Something needed to be said.

The Nephew seemed to think so, too.

He was also in the Duty-Free Shop, wearing a velour track-suit, fur-lined leather slippers, and a neck pillow with built-in headphones, and was making his way over to the young men ahead of Prin. Rae was pushing a full shopping cart behind him. Prin tried to catch her eye but she was busy making faces with a little kid strapped into a stroller while his mother sampled skin creams. The kid was stamping his feet against the stroller's bottom strap, which activated the red lights in the heels of his shoes. He was extremely proud and was rewarding himself with scoops of goldfish crackers after each stomp. Rae's bright face told him she wanted to see more and more and more.

Meanwhile, The Nephew was lecturing the impressed young men. What kind of vulgar morons bought rum? He took them over to a coolly lit display of Japanese single-malt whisky. Tall, thin young women in elegant taupe hijabs were positioned every-where, smiling and faintly nodding with an air that suggested they were happy to help without touching anything or being touched.

Prin left. He went next door to a gift shop. He wanted to pick something up for Molly and the girls. He had planned to find them gifts in the famous markets of the old city. The leather shops of Dragomans turned out such beautiful purses, the world's most splendid women, from Josephine Bonaparte to Angelina Jolie, had owned one. But no one from the government complex had been willing to take him there before he left. They assured him it was safe to go, totally safe, that there were no problems at all, safe totally; but still, even if it were that safe, which it was, this was true, why take a chance? Totally safe.

In the back of the airport gift shop, amid T-shirts and fuzzy stuffed camels and dates, he found a small selection of soft, deep burgundy leather purses, each tagged with a picture of the saffron tented market where they had been made, for centuries, according to secret, family-held traditions. Prin read the fine print at the bottom of the tag. Made in China. He could cut off the tags before giving them to the girls. He picked up four, then made it five, then went back to four.

On a shelf full of snow-globe mosques that you could shake into sandstorms, Prin found two bookends modelled after the chapel in the mountain. He picked one up. It was heavy, far too heavy to take home in his luggage. He'd have to carry it himself, the whole way. He'd keep it on his lap in the plane. Right where her sleeping leg would never lie again. Nothing would be enough to merit her mercy, her forgiveness. But this was something he could do, and if she took it from him and threw it in the trash, or dropped it on his toe, or told him to keep holding it until it was time for him to be buried with it, he would accept this. He would accept anything, just so long as she responded.

He called her again.

Straight to voicemail. Again.

He brought the purses and bookend to the counter and left them there to go look for a book. Then he went back and picked up the bookend. The whole point was to carry it the entire time, from now until he saw Molly.

And he neither wanted nor deserved any Simon's help.

Prin walked past breath mints and magazines and a device-charging station where a large man checked his phone while standing at a painful-looking angle for a large man. A clerk stood beside him, stooped in smiling replica.

Prin made his way to the books section. Other than a few local histories, here was standard airport reading: popular novels and prize-sticker novels; biographies and memoirs and manifestos of retired generals and presidential hopefuls and tech gurus and tech titans and tech prophets and tech prophets of doom; leadership books that promised to "unleash" some things and "conquer" others; histories of the world in seven volcanos, in fifteen paperclips, in five Steven Spielberg movies, in a recipe for jambalaya; books that promised all life's lessons could be learned from Homer and Virgil and Zuzu's Petals and marmots and earthworms.

Prin flipped through a few. He found his situation in some books and didn't want to read on, or he failed to find it, and wondered what was the point of distracting himself. He'd fly home with nothing to read. He would tell her that, too.

Prin returned to the counter, paid for everything at an automated checkout, and declined to have the bookend boxed. He put the purses in his book bag and left with the bookend in his free hand.

Wende was waiting for him outside the store, drinking a smoothie. She smiled in a sad way and waved in a very small way. Because of his bag and the bookend, he physically couldn't wave back, thank God. But shouldn't he, at least, smile? Wasn't there a seeking-mercy-and-forgiveness in her smile? And if he was so desperate for Molly to respond to him, couldn't he at least offer to Wende what—

"GUARDS! STOP HIM! SOMEONE! STOP HIM!"

Prin turned around and put the bookend down to find his receipt. It must have looked like he'd just walked out of the store with it.

But the clerk wasn't pointing at Prin. She was pointing at a man in a drab cloak and black balaclava who was jogging towards Wende. He stopped and pulled up a long black gun and shot her and she fell with a look on her face like someone had just pulled a giant stitch out of her back. Then he stepped close and shot her some more. He stumbled backwards with the recoil and the gun slipped down and he rubbed his shoulder. He looked around and began jogging again.

More men, many more men in drab cloaks and black bala-clavas now filled the terminal, guns firing, their barrels waving away screaming hijab women and their shrieking, clutching children. The gunmen jogged around shooting and people were screaming and glass was shattering and everything and every-one was falling down everywhere.

Running backwards Prin bumped against the wall beside the Duty-Free shop. There was a big potted plant on the floor. He slipped behind it. The plant was thick and bushy. How long until they found him? He smelled burning and hot metal and sulfur and piss. His crotch was soaking.

He tried to say a Hail Molly for Wende's life and another that he be spared but couldn't remember because a gunman was there, *right there*. He shot up the liquor bottles in the Duty-Free. The sacrilegious manspreader sprinted out and tripped on someone's luggage. He got up and the gunman shot him. He walked over and saw the bikini blonde rippling across the front of the writhing young man's long white shorts, and he shot and shot. Then he just stared down at the bodies.

When the gunman looked up he'd see Prin. His head was pure and empty. So was Prin's. Not it wasn't. His only thought was that Wende was dead and now Molly need never have known. Damn. Just then he felt something open up near his chest. In it. All this noise of gunfire and casings dropping on the floor—had he been shot without noticing? No. So what was this sudden blackness come into him? It was that in these, his final moments, that, *that*, had been his only thought. Not for Wende's soul. Not for Molly's mercy. Not for his girls, or for all of them in the life to come, a life without him, and for him a life without them, but that it was unfair he had told Molly something that now never needed to have been told.

Also: God, how dare You ask me to come here, for this!

Damn You.

Damn me for damning You.

Damn me for all of this dare.

The gunman looked up and Prin pressed against the wall and sobbed and held his breath, but then another gunman ran past and called and the nearby gunman stepped over the dead young man and slipped a little and ran on.

Prin sobbed for air and almost made a sign of the cross but then jumped back against the wall at the sound of sirens coming on—bells ringing and also a metallic whining. There wasn't as much gunfire immediately around him. Suddenly, there was no noise at all. The lights went out and everything was grey-brown. Prin peeked out from behind the potted plant. No one moved. Here was his chance.

To do what, exactly?

His ears were ringing and he took off his glasses and wiped his face.

Hide in a better place than behind a potted plant, at least.

Eyes going everywhere, heart gorging his throat, he held his breath and stepped out and they starting shooting and he jumped back and breathed out hard. But this time the gunfire wasn't near him. He held his breath and stepped out again and shook and convulsed with the noises and ran into the Duty-Free shop.

Kicking glass and shells, he slipped through broken bottles and amber puddles and goldfish and blood from a limp, velour-covered arm stretched out on the floor. The Nephew's. Prin looked around for Rae. Then he almost tripped, dear Jesus he'd stepped into an empty baby stroller fallen on its side.

Not goldfish. Goldfish crackers. Those were a child's gold-fish crackers. *That child's.* Prin stopped and crouched and listened for crying. In vain. Then, crying, he looked for a body. Blunt-shock wrong was Wende's death and who knows how many more in the airport. Sad, tragic, wrong.

But who shoots a baby in a stroller?

Then, closer to the back of the store in the murk-light, he saw bright red flashing lights. Coming from a shoe, an empty shoe. Hunched over and now smelling alcohol and perfume, Prin went looking for the child. A little boy standing all by himself biting his fingers raw so no bad men could hear him crying. He checked behind a dark, wooden display of single malt Scotches. There was no one hiding there.

Someone must have picked up the child. Someone good, God, let it be someone good who picked up the child and ran from here and be safe now and at the hour of her death, and let that hour be long and far from here and now, amen.

Rae.

Rae had the child.

Gunfire again.

This time it came from closer. There was yelling, too. Why were they yelling now? Was it even them? Was it the Dragomans army? Would they know Prin was innocent? He was brown and he had a beard but he had his passport and didn't he have a rosary his mother made him always carry a rosary when he travelled but he didn't tell her this time but wasn't there one in his jacket pocket and he went to check but then gunfire started again. This time it was coming from the far side of the terminal. The yelling became more frantic, and then suddenly everything went silent. There was a scratchy walk-ie-talkie noise and then everyone started shooting everywhere.

He looked around the shop and saw a plain door in a far corner. An exit? Prin ducked down and held his breath and ran there and pushed through and the door closed right after him and now he was standing in the dark.

37

HE TOOK OUT his phone and turned on the flashlight and waved it around—rack after rack of bottles, liquor and perfume, and barrels and boxes of candy. There was no back door to the outside. He went down one aisle and then turned off the flashlight and made his way to a back corner. If they found him here, he had nowhere to go. He got up and moved into a middle aisle. His ears were ringing, clanging like someone had run a railroad crossing through his brain!

He sat down behind a fortress wall of giant Toblerone bars. He hung his head down into his lap and tried to say the "Now I Lay Me Down to Sleep" prayer. Prin wept like a little boy.

He stopped crying, jerked up, and checked his phone. He still had data coverage and 20 percent battery life.

God please, let her respond now!

The call didn't go through.

He could at least write something to Molly, something to the girls. Only he couldn't type. His fingers were wet with sweat and crying; his shirt was drenched and the screen wouldn't respond to his tapping, except in the upper corner. He couldn't even type "love u," so Prin sent Molly a blank message from this, the dark end of his life.

He hoped, he prayed she would understand he'd tried, he'd tried very hard. He'd always tried very hard. And he was sorry. So sorry. Because what exactly had he tried so hard to do?

Christ, was it only to say look at me, everybody; look at me, going everywhere? Look at me.

A long time, maybe an hour, maybe two hours after the message finally showed as sent, Prin heard gunshots from much closer, from inside the Duty-Free shop. More bottles shattered and then the door to the stockroom opened and right away slammed shut and Prin couldn't move, he couldn't move, even if he wanted to he couldn't move. Something was pressing him firmly against the Toblerone. The pressure let up when he heard weeping, terrified weeping, another man's terrified weeping.

Someone else was hiding with him in the stockroom now.

He had to get the person away from the door before they heard him in here. Both of them, in here. Prin stood up and stepped into the aisle and turned on his phone's flashlight.

"Quick, come back here," he said.

The man looked over and sucked back his crying and jumped to his feet and banged against the wall and then against his chest. One of the gunmen!

Prin dropped his phone but the light was shining up at him and the man came charging down the main aisle towards him and he was too close and he pulled a gun out from the back of his pants and Prin asked God please to watch over them and then he dropped to his knees and, closing his eyes, felt a force surge through his body and flame through his heart as to his killer he declared,

"*La illah ila Allah, Muhammad Rasul Allah!*"

The man stopped short. He considered Prin for a moment. This was a very long moment. He swallowed. They both swallowed. The gunman motioned for Prin to get up and step back then he stepped forward and picked up Prin's phone and flashed it at him.

"Wait, bro, you're one of us?" he asked.

Tears streaming, Prin opened his eyes.

"*La illah ila Allah, Muhammad Rasul Allah!*" he said.

The young man turned off the flashlight and put Prin's phone in a pocket and put his gun away and pulled down his balaclava and reached out in the dark and put his free hand on Prin's shoulder.

"It's okay, it's okay. *La illah ila Allah, Muhammad Rasul Allah*. It's cool. We're on the same team, bro," he said.

Prin stood up and wiped the tears from his eyes. Just then, emergency lights went on at far intervals across the stockroom ceiling. In the dim yellow light Prin looked at the young man, who was also wiping tears from his big brown eyes. He was trying to do this quickly.

Prin wanted to scream and scream and scream and scream. But instead he listened. In his head, passing through his ears still ringing he could hear two children, two of his children, playing piano. It was a duet they had written themselves, for that year's spring concert. Philomena and Chiara had sat at far ends of the same bench, one playing high notes that were answered by the other playing low notes. They called their song "It's the end. No it's not: The Sisters' Duelling Duet."

The song consisted of this argument, which came out as three high notes followed by three matching low notes. The song was sixty seconds long and the game of it was to get the last notes in before time was up. They had played it together, had played it with each other and against each other for hours that spring, sixty seconds at a time.

Prin's sixty seconds weren't up yet.

Here and now, this was the man he had to be.

"Wait. If we're on the same team, bro, why are we both hiding back here instead of going out there to, er, to wage holy jihad?" Prin asked.

"But—"

"Fuck buts. Why were you just crying? Why aren't we both out there, killing the, the damned infidels?" Prin asked.

The young man's face was blank. He stepped back. He put up his hands.

"I know, I just, this is my first time, bro, okay? And I just made a move, I was actually coming up along the side to take down some of the security guards but then I dropped my gun, I mean my gun jammed and I didn't want to use my back-up, whatever. So I ducked in here just to regroup. But wait. What about you?" he asked.

"What about me?" Prin asked.

Outside, the gunfire was now sporadic, almost bored-sounding.

"But what about you, I asked," he said.

"What do you mean?" Prin asked.

"Well, I don't see you out there. You're just another bad Muslim in an airport, as far as I can tell. How do I know you're truly fighting for the *khilafah?* Something tells me you're not. Something tells me you're just pretending. And I definitely know you pissed your pants. I can smell it, bro. Nasty," he said.

He pulled his balaclava back up over his nose.

"Yeah, bro, how do I know you're even *Mutadayyin Muslim?*" he asked.

Prin snorted and shook his head and stepped up close to the gunman, who stepped back a little.

"Praise Allah and peace be upon His name. Actually I came to Dragomans today for jihad. But how could I tell anyone, when all of this starts just fifteen minutes after I walked off the plane? Bro, who's going to let me interrupt and explain? Think about it. If you hadn't dropped your other gun—"

"It jammed!"

"Right. If it hadn't jammed, what would you have done when you found me in here?" Prin asked.

The young man was pleased with this question.

"Exactly. But Praise Allah and Peace Be Upon His Name, you found me ...We are brothers!" Prin said.

"You took a plane from where? And who are you in touch with here? The fuck invited you? Who said okay? Give me just one name," he said.

"It's complicated," said Prin.

"No it's not, bro," he said.

"Yes it is, okay? The man who invited me works for Dragomans national security. I met him online. I'd tell you his name but then if we're caught——"

"Never going to happen. Trust me. So what's the name?" he asked.

"Rafik. He works inside the government complex, checking cars, VIP infidels, bro," said Prin.

"Never heard of him," he said.

"I believe you, bro. Why won't you believe me?" asked Prin.

"Because I just don't see how you showed up here like this. It's too easy," he said.

"It's complicated," said Prin.

"Bro, this is holy jihad, not fucking Facebook! Look at me. No complications. I took a plane from Boston. Abu Osman al-Helsinki invited me," he said.

"Bro, you don't believe that's a real name, do you? Are you sure you didn't fall for some CIA plot and lead them straight to our brothers?" asked Prin.

"Fuck you, bro! My sheik's the real deal, okay? I haven't met him yet, but he accepted my *bay'a* after I asked for like a year online. And then his followers became my brothers, *my true brothers*, the *muwahhidi* of the new *khilafah*, and they told me I will meet him in person and he will accept my *bay'a* in person right after we purify this airport, *Insha'Allah*. And he said I could also go see my grandmother. Maybe. And what about you?" he said.

"For sure, *Insha'Allah*. Always, *Insha'Allah*. So you grew up in Boston?" asked Prin.

"Nashua, New Hampshire. Kuffar capital of the world, bro. You? Again, stop stalling or I'll un-jam my other gun on your bullshitting ass. What about you?" he asked.

"Toronto," said Prin.

"Blue Jays suck. Raptors suck. TFC is bullshit soccer. Drake's totally annoying," he said.

"Yeah, right, for sure. So what are doing here? Do you want

to lead the way back out?" he asked.

Prin would follow behind him, grab the nearest bottle, and brain him. Why had he dropped the bookend? This man was maybe ten years his junior. The beard made it hard to tell. They were about the same height, the same shape, the same paler shade of brown. But even through his cloak he looked gym-thick in the chest and arms.

But Prin felt the songs and lives of his children surging through his arms.

"For sure. Yeah. Let's do this. But hold up. If you're for real—"

"I'm for real," said Prin.

"Then lead the way," he said.

"But look at me, brother, and look at you. What can I fight the infidels with? You have that other gun, at least," said Prin.

"It's a handgun, bro. I'm kind of in the same situation, right? What am I going to do, out there on my own, when my clip's out?" he asked.

"So what do we do, instead?" asked Prin.

"Obvious. *Salah*," he said.

"Right. *Salah*," Prin said.

"*Salah*," he said.

They stood there in silence.

"You think it's … the right time?" Prin asked.

What was *Salah*? Time to eat? Time to pray?

"Yeah, by now it's probably time for *Zuhr*, noon prayer, I'm guessing," he said.

"Of course! And we pray for victory!" said Prin.

"No, brother. We pray because we pray. But we don't pray for victory, we pray because we pray. That's what we do before Allah, Peace Be Upon His name. Amiright?" he said.

"You're right," said Prin.

38

PRIN FOLLOWED HIM up and down the aisles looking for prayer rugs. The closest thing they found was flattened Danish short-bread cookie boxes.

The young man poured out bottles of Icelandic Glacier Water on their hands for ritual cleansing, paused to calculate something, and then arranged their prayer mats on the floor, towards Mecca. He knelt down on one and motioned Prin to kneel down on the other. They were down on the ground, far away from any head-smashing bottles.

Prin prayed that his mumbling faux Arabic wouldn't be noticed over the other man's praying, never mind the noises outside, which were now just yelling and loudspeaker scratch, the tone suggesting warnings and taunts, demands and threats, back and forth, but no gunshots.

There were definitely more voices coming from one side than the other.

Which was down to a few fighters? And how long before whoever came back this way?

Prin needed more time. He had no idea how long these prayers went on. He was shaking with the idea that the other man would hit him with something while his head was down. He reared back and stood up and let out a choked sob.

"I can't do this. Brother, I can't pretend any longer," Prin said.

The young man sprang to his feet and got in his face.

"I fucking knew it! I knew it! You're no *Mutadayyin Muslim!*" he said.

The young man jabbed a finger into Prin's forehead. Then he jabbed his own a few times.

"Your forehead is smooth, bro. You never pray. Check out mine. Five times a day, every day, bro," he said.

"Yes. I see and I can feel the difference. You're totally right. I don't pray. My father, my father, what an evil man, he refused to teach me the faith, my whole life. He never let us go to mosque, he refused to keep halal, he laughed and ate steak and Snickers bars in front of his brothers and our cousins all day during Ramadan. I know nothing of the faith, brother, not even the prayers, only what I could find online," Prin said.

"What sites?" he asked.

"What sites?" Prin asked.

"Yeah. What sites do you go to? You can't just Google 'I want to be a better Muslim,' bro—"

"Actually, yes you can. That's what I did. That's how it started," Prin said.

"Well, okay, you're right. I actually started with Twitter: hashtag headmeat. But then what sites did you go to? *Dabiq?* What sheikhs do you follow? Yacoub? And don't just say 'Yeah, those ones,' because I know you're bullshitting," he said.

"Listen, I don't know how long we're going to be in here or what's going to happen next. What I found online was *La illah ila Allah, Muhammad Rasul Allah*, and I visited enough places to know I would find His Mercy in coming here to Dragomans and waging jihad, *Insha'Allah*. I don't know if in His Mercy Allah will forgive me for following my father's ways for so long, but I can at least try. Amiright?" Prin said.

The young man studied Prin. Then he giggled and shook his head.

"Bro, you and me both. My dad was the most anti-Muslim Muslim in all of America. He always said his favourite sheikh was the Iron Sheikh. You know, the wrestler? I came here more or less just like you. Some other stuff was going on, but yeah, basically, we're the same," he said.

"Yes, we're the same. And we found each other, thanks be to Allah and Peace Upon His Name. So, what else was going on?" Prin asked.

He was now using the same voice he found when students came to him with their stories, seeking extensions for papers.

"Hold up. We need to complete *Zuhr*," he said.

"Right. Please, teach me the way," Prin said.

They pressed their heads down and prayed.

When they finished, the young man sat up, stood, then carefully removed the Danish blue cardboard prayer mats from the concrete floor and placed it on a nearby shelf. Prin did the same.

"Who knows how long we'll be in here, right?" he said.

"Right. So, you were saying you had some stuff going on, before you came over?" Prin asked.

"Yeah, stuff, you know? Like I said, my grandmother, who actually lives in Dragomans, she's really sick. But other stuff, too," he said.

"Yeah, me too. But hey, tell me more. Like you said, we might be here for a while, depending on what's going on outside. It's already been at least an hour, right?" Prin said.

"Probably even longer, bro. So do you think we need a plan if one of the army men come in here? Or if some *kuffar* tourist tries to come in to hide?" he said.

"You'll know what to do," Prin said.

"Right on," said the young man.

"So come on, we're brothers, what's been going on?" Prin asked.

"No man, it's all shit and none of it matters because now I'm all for Allah and Peace Be Upon His name," he said.

"Me too. You want me to go first? What I was dealing with, how I ended up here? My name's Kareem, by the way," Prin said.

"Okay. I'm Dawud. My buddies used to call me Dave. So did my dad and my brothers," he said.

"But your true brothers call you Dawud," Prin said.

"That's right, Kareem," he said.

"So, Dawud, you want to hear my story?" asked Prin.

"Nothing else to do until they come for us, right? Whether it's our brothers or the army guys? There's a rumour that American Special Forces guys are here too. Imagine if one of them came in here. Right?" he said.

Dawud swallowed hard when he said that.

A doe-eyed kid with gym muscles and a peach-pit prayer bump on his forehead.

"Well whoever's out there, they've all stopped shooting. And there's not as much talking as before. What do you think that means, Kareem?" he asked.

"It could mean anything. For now, I think it means we wait here, wait for a sign of what we should do next. It'll come, *Insha'Allah*," Prin said.

"*Insha'Allah*. And I don't want to use my gun in here and tip off our location. We should have bottles with us," he said.

39

THE TWO OF them walked around until they found big bottles of Absolut and Canadian Club.

"Now we're ready," he said.

"That's right. But also, sorry, I know this is going to sound lame, but I'm starving," Prin said.

"Me too, for sure!" he said.

He tapped the billowy sides of his cloak.

"Bro, I've been here two weeks and never mind Ramadan, I've lost twenty pounds, I swear. If my grandmother saw me—"

Bad idea, thinking of his grandmother just now. He shook his head free of her and kept going.

"Listen, I'll eat almost anything other than chickpeas and dates and pita, bro. That's basically all they give you when you join. Even for Iftar at night, that's it! Also, this nasty yoghurt drink that I'm pretty sure has gone bad but they think it's supposed to taste that way," he said.

"Well, I guess I'll get my fill of that food, if we make it out of here, *Insha'Allah*," Prin said.

"Yeah yeah, *Insha'Allah*," he said.

"*Insha'Allah*. So, what's wrong with some M&M's right now? Do you think there's a hadith authorizing the eating of the infidel's rations during a time of war? You'd know better than I would," Prin said.

"For sure. It's not like they're bacon M&M's, right?" he said.

Prin fist-bumped Dawud and they went down another aisle—soaps, colognes and perfumes, hair-dryers with engines by Porsche, Braun electric razors, deluxe antimacassars—and then another aisle, and another, until at last they found a giant Rubik's cube set-up of M&M's. Each tore open a carton and took out a bag the size of a small pillowcase.

Prin downed a handful for Dawud's every two. Everything was quiet but for the sound of happy crunching. After a little while, they nodded at each other.

"So, what do you think, does this make sense, what we're doing right now?" Prin asked.

Dawud paused between handfuls. He looked annoyed.

"Wait, you said there was a hadith. Now you're saying eating M&M's during jihad is haram?" he said.

"Actually I asked *you* if there's a hadith. But I'm sure there is. I just mean, the two of us sitting back here like this, eating snacks and talking, while who-knows-what's happening to our brothers right now. You think that's okay?" Prin asked.

"Listen, we're not going to just give up, right, bro? We can't. Even if we wanted to, we can't. We can't, we can't, we can't … and we don't want to! So let's just say our brothers have all gone to the paradise of the martyrs—"

"*Insha'Allah*," Prin said.

"Yeah yeah, *Insha'Allah*, and so, well, we know we're going to join them, right?" he said.

"Right," Prin said.

"So, whether it happens in five minutes or five hours, what's the difference?" he asked.

"Well, I'd rather spend more time in paradise than sitting here, like this, right?" Prin said.

"Sure, but bro, it's not all about you, right? I mean, how much better if they think we're all dead and then do a sweep back here and we take down a few more of them? To me, that's totally worth waiting a few extra hours before … paradise," he said.

"You're right. You're younger than me, brother, but very wise. Thank you," Prin said.

The young man shrugged off the compliment, unconvincingly.

"So then, how should we wait for them to come for us?" Prin asked.

This entire time, Prin had been making infinitesimal shifts along the floor towards the whisky bottle near him.

"Look, it's been days since I've had a chance to talk like this, with a brother. Most of the others only speak in Arabic, and I can get by or whatever, but even the brothers from England or wherever won't really speak to you in English. And they're always texting people back home and chatting with fat ugly *kuffar* French girls looking for boyfriends. They're not looking to hear anyone's story here or, whatever, make any friends. So it's just, you know, good to talk like this," he said.

"I agree," said Prin.

"Then what's your story, bro? Tell me how you got here," he said.

"Okay. So here goes. This won't be easy, okay?" Prin said.

"Bro, Hadith 54," he said.

"I'm not going to lie to you. I have no idea what Hadith 54 says," Prin said.

"Bro! You just made yourself Hadith 54 legit! It's the one that says we just need to keep on telling the truth, all the way to Allah, Peace Be Upon His Name, and if we don't …"

"If we don't …"

"We burn. But not the good burn, like at the end of a beast set in the gym or … taking out *kuffars*, but, you know, the other place," he said.

"Hell," Prin said.

"Get with the true wording, Bro! We call it *al-Nar*," he said.

"Got it. Thanks, I'm going to try my best—"

"No you're not! You're going to tell the truth! Hadith …"

"54. Yes. Right. So obviously I'm older than you, and come to this not knowing a lot except this: a few months ago, I was diagnosed with cancer," Prin said.

"Oh! Bro, that sucks," he said.

He tapped himself in the chest twice and then reached over and shared a fist bump with Prin.

"Thanks. It's okay. I'm here now, right? And that's for one reason only. The night before my surgery, I prayed to God— didn't even call Him Allah Peace Be Upon His Name back then, that's how far away I was—that I would do something important with my life, if He let me live. And that wasn't going back to teaching high-school English to anti-Muslim infidels. *Kuffars*," Prin said.

"You're a teacher?" he asked.

"I used to be. Now I've come here," Prin said.

"And what's your wife think about it?" he asked.

"My wife?" Prin said.

"Fourth finger, left hand," he said.

"Bro, you should be in intelligence, not just a regular fighter. But, well, actually I'm not married. I don't have a wife," Prin said.

He pulled off his wedding ring and studied it in his palm. He squeezed his eyes shut.

"So I read online that the border guards stop you from coming in if you fit the profile—single brown male, 19-45. I bought a fake ring so I could get past passport control. But now that you've already started the purification of Dragomans, I guess I won't have to worry about passport checks," Prin said.

He tossed his wedding ring down the aisle.

"Funny you said what you said," he said.

"What?" Prin asked.

"That I should be in intelligence," he said.

"Why?" Prin asked.

He shrugged and tried to hide his smile.

He didn't try very hard.

"Bro, come on, tell me," Prin said.

"I really shouldn't. I'm not supposed to tell anyone," he said.

"So, can you at least tell me when we're both in the martyr's paradise?" Prin asked.

"For sure, 100 percent," he said.

"So what's the difference, telling me five hours earlier?" Prin asked.

He nodded, conceding the point.

Also, he desperately wanted to concede this point.

"So, I've already been sent out as advance intelligence on a mission. I set it up, but it didn't work out, which is why the Sheikh decided on the airport, instead," he said.

"You can't say what the mission was?" Prin asked.

"You'll keep this to your death?" he asked.

"*Insha'Allah*, Hadith 54," Prin said.

"So for sure? 100 percent?" he asked.

"That's what it means, right bro?" Prin said.

"Right. Okay. So I had to pretend I was a business-development guy for startups. That's how I got a meeting with this retarded Silicon Valley-wannabe Dragomans douchebag politician who's all set up fancy in the big government complex and thinks he's Steve Jobs or whatever. I said my startup was working on a new kind of security-tracking tab and that got me in behind the walls for a meeting, bro; behind the walls, no problem. Only the politician couldn't meet with me and instead I had to meet with these ... women," he said.

Prin spat.

"Exactly. These two women, their hijabs weren't even tight, and they asked to see a demo and I'm like 'sure, sure,' but wow, what a place, can I get a tour first? and they were so stupid they showed me around and so I took all these notes about the complex, the number of guards I saw, that kind of thing," he said.

"And you didn't connect with my guy Rafik, seriously?" Prin asked.

"That's right. But maybe he knew something and told the Sheikh it wasn't the right time. Who knows? I didn't hear anything about that, only that it was called off and then we were supposed to be going into the big market in the old city this morning, but then that was called off, and suddenly we're all in delivery trucks, going to this fake Christian chapel in the middle of some mountain, but that was called off too and so then we came to the airport. And then it was on, bro, it was *on*. Big-time, like every video game and blessing of the Prophet rolled into one. So fuck, yeah, I did, I actually did it," he said.

"Did what?" Prin asked.

"You know what I mean. Now your turn," he said.

"Wait. Dawud, brother, what did you do?" Prin asked.

"I purified this land of an infidel," he said.

His voice was joyless and flat and metallic.

"What kind?" Prin asked.

"Some skinny slut. She dropped her smoothie when I hit her and some of it got on my shoes. See?" he said.

"Yes, I, I see. But, she wasn't, I mean, how do you know she was a ..."

"What, a slut? Well, first of all, she was totally uncovered! And her shirt's undone all the way, tight pants, jewellery. Kind of obvious, bro," he said.

"Okay ... Praise, p-praise be unto Allah and peace be upon His name ... Way, um, way to go, bro," Prin said.

"Thanks," he said.

"But only one?" Prin asked.

"One more than you, bro. But that's right. I had, well, whatever," he said.

"You had what?" Prin asked.

"Well, so I had a pretty clean shot at this other chick. Chinese," he said.

"And?"

"I TOLD YOU! MY GUN JAMMED!" he said.

"Okay, okay. Easy. Sorry, all's good," Prin said.

"So cancer, right? Is that what woke you up to the call?" he asked.

"Yeah. So like I told you already, Dawud, I had cancer, I prayed to Allah, Peace Be Upon His Name, I made a promise to Allah, Peace Be Upon His Name, and my cancer was cured, and so I came here," he said.

"I don't believe you," he said.

His voice was again metallic and flat.

"That's just too easy. No one's story is that easy," he said.

"Oh, so now you're cool with complicated? What about your story?" Prin asked.

"What about it?" he asked.

"Did your gun really jam, or did you get scared and run in here?" Prin asked.

He punched Prin in the mouth. Prin's head snapped back against the stock shelf. He spat out a tooth in a gobby little balloon of blood. His face throbbed. His heart was banging all the way through to his fattening lip now and he strained to hear anything else. Still no gunfire, no calling for help, no barking orders and threats and taunts.

Was it all over?

How much longer before someone checked the stockroom?

Could he keep this going for long enough?

Or would he have to try with the bottle?

Shaking his head and holding both hands to his bleeding mouth, he writhed closer to the bottle.

"I'm sorry, brother. I'm truly sorry. Forgive me," Prin said.

"Not until you tell me the truth, bro. The more I think about this, the less it makes sense. You're cured of cancer and then just walk off a plane, not knowing anyone here, and not even a Dragomani yourself, but you're all ready to make jihad? Nope. You better start proving yourself legit *Mutadayyin Muslim* or else I'm going to do more than just punch you in the face," he said.

"You want the total truth?" Prin asked.

"100 percent," he said.

"Then first just tell me your gun didn't jam—"

"You want me to prove it on your ass right now?" he asked.

"Trust, bro. I trust you. Trust me. I can tell you're holding something back. Get it out. This is the time and place. Just get it out," Prin said.

The young man trembled and held his face in his hands. Prin reached for the Canadian Club but then Dawud looked up and he was crying.

"I couldn't do it. The white chick was easy. I didn't even see her face until after she was dead. Super slutty, for sure. So I moved on and I saw this little Chinese lady and, and, easy shot, but she was holding this little kid wearing those shoes that flash and I used to have those shoes and they were both crying and looking around and yes they were infidels and yes they were an easy shot, easy shot, easy ..."

"But you didn't do it," Prin prayed.

"I didn't," he said.

He began sobbing, head down low, perfect, and Prin grabbed the bottle. But he couldn't do it. Not like this. Because of this man, *this man,* Rae and the child were alive.

"Bro, you showed mercy, and Allah Peace Be Upon His Name is merciful, and Allah Peace Be Upon His Name is pleased," Prin said.

Dawud looked up and wiped his face.

"Yeah ... we'll see. So tell me your full truth. Do it. Do it now," he said.

"Okay. I didn't just come here straight from getting cured of my cancer. I went somewhere else, first," Prin said.

"Where did you go?" he asked.

"Does it really matter? I'm here now, right, and ready for jihad," Prin said.

"Bullshit. You're a fraud," he said.

"I'M NO FRAUD!" Prin said.

Dawud sat back a little, closer to his vodka bottle.

"Sorry," Prin said. "Look, I'm no fraud, bro. I'm no fraud. I'm not. But I will admit to you, I am in need of purification because of all that I did before I came here. I knew I would be purified by jihad. I knew this. I believed it, thanks to Allah and Peace Be Upon His Name. Didn't the 9/11 martyrs go to Las Vegas before they took the planes? They did!" Prin said.

"Tell me right now, bro. What did you do?" he asked.

"Give me back my phone and I will show you," Prin said.

"Yeah right," he said.

He took Prin's phone out of his pocket and considered its home screen.

"Wait. So you said you weren't married but then who are—"

"My brother's kids. My nieces," Prin said.

"Cute girls," Dawud said.

Prin lunged and grabbed the phone and the next thing he knew he was chest down on the ground, the other man's knee in his back. Dawud bent back his wrist and he dropped the phone. The other man picked it up, stood back, and took out his gun.

"I am at your mercy, brother," Prin said.

"No shit," he said.

"No, I mean, please, here's the truth. Fine. See for yourself what filth I touched before coming here in search of purity, *Insha'Allah*," Prin said.

"The fuck you saying?" asked Dawud.

"Just, just put 6791 for the passcode and then open my VaultTok app ... and look for the picture of, of, the slut," Prin said.

Dawud immediately found the picture of Wende's chest. He squatted down, put aside his gun, and with his free hand rubbed his forehead and expanded the image. He was muttering something, and whatever it was, it was no prayer, no curse.

He'd forgotten Prin was even there.

Prin reached for his Canadian Club and swung down just as Dawud dropped the phone and came up with his Absolut.

40

"HELP! PLEASE, CAN you hear me out there? HELP! I'm trapped in here with a terrorist! Can any of you understand English?"

"*Min a'nat? Min a'anat?*" asked a Dragomans soldier.

"My name is Princely St. John Umbiligoda, and I'm a Canadian citizen and help! I'm trapped in here with a terrorist! Please! Please! Someone help me!"

"Is he armed?" called out an American megaphone voice.

"Yes! And he tried to kill me with a liquor bottle but I hit him first and then I tied him up and I've been waiting in here until it was safe to come out. But please, God, he's waking up and I think he's going to get loose. Please! Please, can I come out?"

"Place your hands above your head and come out, slowly," said the American megaphone voice.

"There's no time! Please don't shoot me! Please! I will come out holding my passport, my Canadian passport, above my head with my good hand, okay? My other arm's injured. And then please send your men in here to get him before he breaks free and blows us all up!"

"Come out! There will be guns aimed at you and if you do not do exactly as you are told, or if you make any unnecessary movements, you will be shot. Do you understand? You will be shot. Do you understand?"

"YES! Please, just let me out! Don't shoot me! Shoot him!"

"Come out, now."

"Okay, I'm coming out. I'm coming out. Don't shoot me, please!"

Prin was screaming and screaming.

But no one could hear him.

Wearing Prin's jacket and holding Prin's passport, Dawud walked out of the stockroom into spotlights and men yelling and loudspeakers screeching.

Behind him, gagged and wearing Dawud's balaclava and cloak, Prin stood up. His hands were bound with packing-tape. He staggered. He was dizzy and his head was throbbing and wet and the wet was something thick and coming down near one of his eyes, onto his cheek.

Smelled like metal and meat.

Blood.

Eyes stinging, he looked ahead. He saw the gun tucked in the small of Dawud's back.

The soldiers couldn't see.

They couldn't see how close the gun was to the hand he had pressed along his side. Dawud was about to shoot them.

Original Prin lurched out of the stockroom and into the Duty-Free shop, his bound hands held out in front of him, shaking his head so the balaclava would come off but it wouldn't and the whirring made him dizzy and he stumbled into a table of bottles that fell and broke and more blood came down the side of his face and he was screaming and screaming and sucking in his belly and straining for when they shot him.

The American megaphone voice told him to stop right there. The voice told the other man to stop right there. The voice told both men to get down on their knees.

Prin knelt. Dawud knelt. Then the American told them to lie down flat on the floor. Prin fell forward. Broken glass pierced his legs, his stomach. Wet. Whisky and metal and blood smells. Dawud did not lie down. From his knees, hand reaching for gun, hand reaching for gun, Dawud yelled at the men to shoot the terrorist shoot the suicide bomber shoot and save them all and they were yelling to lie down lie down right now there was yelling everywhere, everyone.

"DOWN ON THE FLOOR!"

Dawud almost had the gun. But they were all screaming and could not hear Prin's screaming. How to show that he wasn't the suicide bomber, that he was true Prin, that the other was about to kill them?

How, Lord? How to show?

Then a great wind came, a blowing in his ears, a rushing through him. With him. In him. He closed his eyes. His body filled and he breathed and he heard and he did not ask God why.

It was the end, and he was not alone. But then the great wind left him.

But he was not alone.

He never was.

He opened his eyes and saw this man with a gun get up from his knees running and crying God is great God is great but the world is the world and the world became fire.

It's the end. No it's not.

No it's not?

The shooting had stopped. Phones were ringing. Glass kept breaking. Men kept yelling. Children were crying.

Children.

No, it's not.

No, it's not.

No, it's not.